Dreams of Jeannie

FIVE STAR

Other Five Star Titles by Catherine Dain:

Follow the Murder
Angel in the Dark
Darkness at the Door
Death of the Party

Dreams of Jeannie

and Other Stories

Catherine Dain

Five Star • Waterville, Maine

Additional copyright information on page 219.

This collection of stories is a work of fiction. Names, characters, places, and incidents are either the product of the author's imagination, or, if real, used fictitiously.

First Edition
First Printing: July 2003

Published in 2003 in conjunction with Tekno Books and Ed Gorman.

Set in 11 pt. Plantin by Elena Picard.

Printed in the United States on permanent paper.

Library of Congress Cataloging-in-Publication Data

Dain, Catherine.
Dreams of Jeannie and other stories / Catherine Dain.
p. cm.
"Five Star first edition titles"—T.p. verso.
ISBN 0-7862-5440-8 (hc : alk. paper)
1. Detective and mystery stories, American. I. Title.
PS3554.A32D74 2003
813′.54—dc21 2003052926

Dreams of Jeannie

and Other Stories

Table of Contents

Dreams of Jeannie

A New Age Mystery

Mariana Morgan has been the protagonist of two New Age mystery novels, one (Angel in the Dark) *in which she had to develop her psychic powers to solve her husband's murder, and a second that picks up her life after she has become a professional psychic, when she uses those powers to search for her missing brother and solve a murder that occurs at Enchantment, the metaphysical store where she works. The events of this story take place shortly after the time of* Darkness at the Door.

"I am so tired of clients insisting that their dreams of a terrorist attack are clairvoyant," Mariana snapped. "The dreams are the body's attempts to call attention to stress. Personal stress combined with the anxiety of the collective unconscious, that's all. How long is it going to take before we go on to the next fad?"

She leaned against the jewelry counter, hoping for some attention, but Deirdre was devoting herself to polishing earrings and didn't look up. Deirdre ran Enchantment, a small store and metaphysical center, with impressive attention to detail.

"Well, the sleeping-with-Bill dreams persisted a couple of years after his presidency ended," Deirdre answered calmly. "So I think we're going to be hearing about terrorists for a while. You'd better find a way to deal with your own stress so you can nod and listen when your clients express theirs. Right now, I suggest you go outside, take a psychic shower, clear your chakras, and come in again."

Mariana straightened up, uncertain whether to follow Deirdre's advice or argue with her. Clearing her chakras before the next client arrived for a psychic reading was a good idea. But she had half an hour, and arguing felt more satisfying.

"Why don't you hold a workshop on dreams?" she asked. "Teach people something instead of letting them muddle through on their own."

"Why don't you?" Deirdre responded.

"Because I don't know enough about dreams. I can give people intuitive help, but I don't know theory, so I can't teach them to help themselves. You can."

"All right." Deirdre finished polishing the silver moon-and-stars earrings she had been working on and removed the polishing glove from her left hand. She looked up at Mariana, giving her full attention. "Tell me what you've been dreaming."

"Not about terrorists." Mariana hesitated. Deirdre waited expectantly. "I dreamed about Tim dying again. And I dreamed about Marion Zimmer Bradley. And I dreamed about an earthquake."

"What did you dream about Marion Zimmer Bradley?" Deirdre was suddenly interested. Although the writer had been dead for several years, her books still sold well. Deirdre had limited shelf space for books, since she had a better mark-up on jewelry, crystals, incense, and other such items for New Age-minded shoppers, but she always had at least one copy of *Mists of Avalon* in stock.

"I dreamed I was standing in line with a group of other women, waiting to hear a great teacher speak. We were outside a temple, and the weather was warm. I could feel the perspiration on my skin. When we were allowed inside, the speaker turned out to be Marion Zimmer Bradley. But she was young, and she wasn't obese," Mariana said.

"How do you feel about Marion Zimmer Bradley?"

"I love her books."

"Okay," Deirdre said, "so either you had an out-of-body experience in which you went to hear her speak in the spirit world because the message in her books means something to you, and you wanted more, or your Higher Consciousness took her form to tell you something."

"I think I was really there. Do astral bodies sweat?"

"Why not? People cry astral tears in their dreams, why not sweat astral beads of perspiration? Do you remember what she told you?" Deirdre asked.

"No."

Deirdre shook her head with impatience.

"Ask for another dream about her, and this time remember. The message might be important—like about writing a great book. And you know why you dream about Tim dying."

"I know. Because I still miss him," Mariana said. "I know he has gone on, which is why he doesn't talk to me as often, but I still miss him. I don't know about asking for a dream about Marion Zimmer Bradley. You're better at asking for dreams than I am. My subconscious doesn't seem to pay attention. Anyway, why would Marion Zimmer Bradley give me a message about a great book?"

"Why not?" Deirdre said again. "Especially if it was just your Higher Consciousness appearing as Marion Zimmer Bradley. Your Higher Consciousness might think it's time for you to use your talent. And if you want to control your dreams, you have to practice."

This time Mariana shook her head.

"Maybe. All right. What about the earthquake?"

"This is Southern California. Wait long enough, there will be an earthquake, and then it will be a clairvoyant dream. Maybe it was nothing more than a truck going by outside, and the rumble became an earthquake in your dream consciousness. Otherwise known as random firing of synapses in your brain. Or maybe something—maybe someone—is coming to shake up your life."

"I could have come up with that myself. And I really don't want my life shaken up, thank you very much. I think I'll go clear my chakras."

Mariana pushed through the glass doors and left the shop. What she saw outside was so unattractive that she almost changed her mind. Minimall parking lots are seldom aesthetically pleasing, and the one in front of Enchantment was no exception. On this day the heavy marine layer, Southern California June gloom extending into July, had added a gray glaze to the picture. Cars, a few people, a street, and another minimall on the other side. All the colors muted, slightly drab. Maybe she could use some change in her life.

She sat down on a bench, took off her sandals so that her feet could feel the energy of the narrow strip of grass between cement and asphalt, and closed her eyes. Visualizing a waterfall of drops all the colors of the rainbow, flowing through her body, clearing her energy centers, helped more than she thought it would. When she opened her eyes, she was ready to go back to the store and see her next client.

"Mariana? I'm Jeannie Cullen, and I'm early. Can we start now?" A woman was standing between the bench and the door, barring Mariana's way. The woman's dark brown hair was wild and frizzed, and her face was flushed from crying. She was wearing a yellow tunic top that didn't go well with her blue and green floral slacks, as if she had dressed in what her hand grabbed from the closet, without paying attention. But even those colors were muted by the gray of the day.

"Of course, Jeannie," Mariana answered, allowing herself a slight twinge of annoyance that her break was over almost before it began. "Come on in the store, let me get a cup of tea, and we'll start."

Deirdre looked up and nodded as they entered.

"Okay?" she asked.

"More or less," Mariana replied.

She slipped behind the counter, dropped a bag of spicy herb tea into a cup, added hot water from the red-topped spout on the dispenser, and slipped back to the customer side.

"Follow me," she said to the distraught woman waiting for her.

Beyond the book section at the back of the store, a hallway led to a combination office and storeroom for Deirdre, two offices that she rented out, the reading room, and a larger room where evening classes were offered.

Mariana ushered Jeannie into the reading room, which wasn't much more than a large closet with a small, round table, two chairs, a framed poster of frolicking dolphins, and a potted plant that somehow managed to sustain itself in fluorescent light.

"I dreamed about a terrorist attack," Jeannie began, before Mariana could even set the timer to thirty minutes.

"Dreams are not necessarily clairvoyant," Mariana said, knowing it would be useless to tell Jeannie that she was the second person that day to come in with a dream of terrorists. Jeannie would take it for confirmation, when it was nothing of the kind. The last client's dream could be easily explained by what was going on in her life. Mariana was certain Jeannie's dream would be the same.

Jeannie glared at her. Mariana knew that she would have to be careful, or the heavy emotion that had caused the flushed face and the swollen eyes would turn to anger.

"You don't understand," Jeannie said. "And I thought you were a psychic. In the dream, my husband was the terrorist."

"I'm sorry," Mariana replied, belatedly switching her attention from herself to her client. "No wonder you're upset. You're right, I didn't take the time to tune in before I answered. What is it you want from me?"

"I want to know what's going on. I know he's involved in something, and now I get this dream that he's a terrorist, planning to blow something up. What is he doing?" Jeannie's eyes began to fill, and her voice broke.

Mariana reached down and grabbed the box of tissues from its place on the floor—there was no room on top of the table—and offered it to Jeannie. Jeannie grabbed two tissues and held them to her eyes.

"Okay," Mariana said, after she had returned the box to the floor. "Here's how we're going to handle it. I want your birthdate, then his first name and birthdate. I'm going to look at your life paths and the path of your relationship, and we'll go from there."

Jeannie glared again, distracted from her tears.

"You think it's about me," she said. "And it isn't. It's my patriotic duty to turn him in, but I need corroboration from somebody before I call the FBI."

"Birthdates," Mariana said calmly.

"I'm a Taurus and he's a Scorpio."

"I don't care about your sun signs. I'm not doing astrology. I want to know your life path cards, the archetypes of the Major Arcana that you're working through. They will help me tune in to the situation. May I have your birthdates?"

Jeannie reluctantly gave her both dates.

"His name is Eric," she added.

Mariana quickly added up the two dates.

"A nine and a one," she said. "You're a Hermit and Eric's a Magician. This has to be a difficult relationship for you under the best of circumstances. You need boundaries, you need a quiet space to get in touch with your own inner truth, and Eric has no concept of the word privacy. He also doesn't have much sense of truth."

"I know that," Jeannie said. "I know he's lying to me. And I know he's a terrorist."

"Doesn't fit the profile," Mariana said, hoping to lighten the mood a little. She didn't like the energy she was picking up from Jeannie, and she didn't like the energy path that she was tuning into as she looked at the two cards, the Hermit and the Magician.

"What kind of psychic are you? You think only Arabs are terrorists?"

"I'm sorry," Mariana said. "We haven't gotten off to a good start. Let's try again." She shuffled the cards and fanned them out on the small table. "Pick six cards, and let's look at your relationship with Eric."

"This is not about my relationship with Eric," Jeannie said, her voice rising. "This is not about me. I want to know what he's doing."

"I understand that. But if you want me to look at him, I have to start by looking at the two of you. That's the way I work," Mariana responded. "You're the one who's here, you're the one who's upset, and I need to look at the energy flow between the two of you. He may not be a terrorist. He could be lying about something else."

"He's a terrorist." Jeannie hesitated, as if she might want to argue, then quickly chose six cards and handed them to Mariana.

Mariana placed them as the base, stem, and petals of a flower, to see the direction of the energy flow. The cards confirmed her own sense that the energy between the two people wasn't good and wasn't going to get better. And there was more. She waited until the images in her head became clearer before she spoke.

"You're partly right," she said. "Eric is involved in something dangerous, and there is someone else involved. But his anger seems personal, not against the government, or anything faceless. You can't talk to him. He won't listen to you. In fact, some of his anger is toward you. The wisest course of action might be for you to move out. Would you like to see what your path looks like if you choose to do that?"

Jeannie shook her head, dismissing Mariana's question. "I know I can't talk to him. I need to talk to the FBI. How can I stop him?"

"You can't. You can't change what he does. You can only protect yourself."

"You are not helping," Jeannie said. Her hands flew around her face, disconnected, then settled back in her lap. "In the dream, he blew something up, something concrete, some kind of building. I wasn't in danger. I think you're wrong. Eric may be angry at me—he's angry at everyone right now—but he isn't going to hurt me."

"What Eric is blowing up is your marriage. Your dream was a metaphor, something that your subconscious was trying to tell you. He may not hurt you physically, but he's hurting you psychologically. You need to get out." Mariana said it flatly. She didn't like telling clients things they didn't want to hear.

"I don't need to get out. I need to get information I can take to the FBI, and you aren't giving me that," Jeannie said. She picked up her bag. "This is useless."

Mariana glanced at the timer.

"We've only used about fifteen minutes," she said. "I'll tell Deirdre to charge you for that."

"Fine."

Jeannie was out the door and halfway down the hall before Mariana caught up with her.

Deirdre barely raised an eyebrow when Mariana explained that Jeannie had called off the reading.

"I couldn't give her what she wanted," Mariana began, once Jeannie had left the store. "She decided to end the reading, and I let her."

"This is the first time a client has walked out on you, but it won't be the last," Deirdre said. "You'll have others. Some will even yell at you. And some of the ones who yell will come back for another reading, but they never apologize. It's all part of the business. Do you want to tell me about it?"

While both psychics kept their clients' secrets where outsiders were concerned, they had agreed when Mariana had first started working at the store that there would be no secrets between the two of them. Mariana thought of Deirdre as the psychic equivalent of a consulting therapist. Although Deirdre was no older than Mariana, both women in their mid-thirties, Deirdre had acknowledged her psychic talents at a younger age and had been a professional for years. For Mariana, the awakening had been later and more difficult, and it was still hard for her to discipline her talents to the constraints of the business.

When Mariana had met Deirdre, shortly after both women had lost their husbands to murder, she hadn't thought they would become friends. She still wasn't sure they were friends. So much about them was different: what they read, what they watched on television, even physical characteristics. But as she looked at Deirdre, with her short, curly blond hair and blue eyes, and thought of herself, with her long, dark hair and dark eyes, she knew that the deep similarities were more important than the surface differences.

"She dreamed her husband is a terrorist. I think it's a metaphor for what's happening in the marriage. And I hope she isn't in danger," Mariana said.

"You could always call David, see what he thinks," Deirdre said.

"Don't, Deirdre. I don't think this is a job for the police, and David would think I wanted to talk to him." Mariana had learned to deflect Deirdre's light jabs, but she wished that Deirdre hadn't mentioned the police detective. There were too many uncertainties in that relationship—if she could even call it that—and she didn't want to deal with them now. Maybe never.

"Then you need to let it go," Deirdre said. "Another psychic shower to clear your chakras, and then get ready for the next client."

"I don't have a next client."

"But you will."

Deirdre was right. Mariana had two more clients that afternoon, neither of which had terrorist dreams. By the time she was through for the day, she was ready to leave all client concerns behind her at the store.

When she reached the small apartment above a garage a

few blocks from the beach, her home in Ventura until she could figure out where to go next, Miles and Ella were waiting to be fed. And Mariana had to feed herself as well. After dinner, she settled down for an evening of watching television, curled up on the bed with the two cats.

She was laughing at an old movie on one of the cable channels when the phone rang.

"Are you watching the news?" Deirdre asked. "If not, turn it on. Your client was murdered. You may want to call David after all."

Deirdre hung up before Mariana could argue with her.

And there it was on the local news. Jean Cullen had been murdered, stabbed to death when she apparently surprised a pair of burglars. Her distraught husband, Eric Cullen, sobbed for the camera. Mariana had been wrong—it was a matter for the police.

Mariana waited until morning, after an almost sleepless night, before she picked up the phone and called David.

He returned her call just as she was getting ready to leave for the store.

"The woman who was murdered last night, Jeannie Cullen," Mariana said. "Her husband did it."

David hesitated, then said, "He couldn't have done it, Mariana. He has an alibi. Eric Cullen owns a custom auto body shop, and for the last couple of weeks he and two other men have been working into the night, restoring a classic Jaguar. They place him at the shop until after ten. Then he stopped for a late dinner, verified by a credit card slip. His wife had been dead for a couple of hours by the time he got home."

"Are you sure? Couldn't the men be covering for him?"

"Believe me, we checked. The spouse is always a suspect until proven otherwise. And burglars don't often break into a home in the middle of the evening when someone is there. Because of that, we'll look at him even harder. But the two men who swore he was working with them seem pretty reliable, and the waitress remembered him, said he didn't seem upset about anything. Why do you think he did it?"

"Because she came to see me yesterday. She said he was a terrorist, plotting something, but I told her she was the one in danger, told her to leave him. I should have called you then," Mariana said.

David laughed gently. "You can call me anytime. But I couldn't have done anything to protect Jean Cullen, you know that."

"You could have had somebody drive by her house last night," Mariana argued.

"But I wouldn't have. You know that, too. We wouldn't have done anything unless she asked for help."

Mariana did know that.

"What happens now?" she asked.

"We investigate it as a burglary that became a murder, just what it appears to be. And don't worry. We'll consider the possibility that Eric Cullen set it up himself, that he hired somebody to do it. Do you have any idea why he might have wanted to get rid of his wife?"

"No. Damn. I don't. She didn't think he was angry at her—she kept calling him a terrorist. I'll tune in later and let you know what I come up with," Mariana said.

"How about over dinner?" David asked.

This was why she hadn't wanted to call him.

"I'll think about it," she said.

"My divorce is final in November. Are you going to make me wait until then?"

"It's not that."

"Then what?"

"We live in such different worlds. I don't think it makes sense to start something that can't go anywhere."

"Would you say that to one of your clients?"

"No, I wouldn't." She would look at the energy flow between the two people, and if it was positive, as she knew it was in this case, she would tell a client not to jump ahead, not to try to guess the end of the relationship at the beginning, because too much can happen in between. People have free will. Take it a step at a time, see what it feels like. "All right. Dinner. But not tonight. I didn't sleep last night, and I'm tired. And I still have to work this afternoon."

"Okay. Tomorrow. I'll pick you up at seven."

Mariana hung up the phone, grabbed the bag that held her cards, said goodbye to the cats, and headed down the stairs to her car. She didn't like being late.

Not that it would have mattered this day. Deirdre was alone when Mariana reached the store, and the only two appointments for readings were scheduled late in the afternoon.

"So what did David say?" Deirdre asked before Mariana even had a chance to put her bag in the reading room and get a cup of tea.

"He said the husband has an alibi," Mariana replied.

"Of course," Deirdre said. "I asked for a dream of Jeannie last night. She realizes now that she was wrong, that she was in danger from her husband. It's some kind of trade, but I don't think she knows the details, even with her enhanced perspective. He's going to do something for someone else, and that's the person who murdered her."

"A dream of Jeannie," Mariana said, smiling in spite of herself.

"But she has dark brown hair," Deirdre said.

"And she spoke to you?"

"Not exactly. Her regret and her husband's anger were feelings that she transmitted. And then I saw an image of something changing hands, and a handshake, and then blood. The blood woke me up. I could be wrong on the interpretation, but I don't think so," Deirdre replied.

"How long have you been able to control your dreams—get what you ask for?" Mariana asked.

"I can't always do it. But I've been working on it for about fifteen years now, and sometimes it works." Deirdre twisted her face into mock annoyance. "It's like everything else connected with the psychic world, though. I can't always get all the information I want. Jeannie didn't tell me anything you could use to convince David that her husband is a murderer."

"Or a terrorist." Mariana lowered her voice. Two women had just entered the shop, heading for the incense display, and she didn't want to discuss the murder with them. "What could this favor be? Do you suppose he really is planning to blow something up?"

"That's as good a favor for murder as any, isn't it?" Deirdre had lowered her voice, too.

Mariana sighed. She felt like a conspirator, the way the two of them had their voices lowered and their heads together. "All right. How do we get more information? Do I read for you, or do you read for me? Or do you want to channel Baba-ji?"

"Well, it gets harder now, because we're both involved to some degree, which makes it harder to get out of the way and let the energy through, as you know." Deirdre said. "And I don't think Baba-ji would be interested in helping out on this one. He'd want to know how this project helps our spiritual growth."

"I should think bringing a murderer to justice is a good

reason to go forward," Mariana said.

"I know you would, but Baba-ji would tell you that the Lords of Karma will take care of Eric Cullen, and that they don't need your help," Deirdre said calmly.

"And so . . ." Mariana prompted.

"And so I think we both ought to ask for dreams of Jeannie. She might get through to you more easily than to me, since you made a psychic connection with her shortly before she died. Let's try that first." The two women customers were standing in front of the cash register, and Deirdre moved away to ring up the purchase.

Mariana wanted something more definitive, but she knew she wasn't going to get it. She needed to prepare for her first client. Jeannie Cullen's murderer would have to wait.

The afternoon dragged for Mariana, with only two readings. Deirdre was busy, though, with a steady stream of customers, so they didn't get a chance to resume the conversation until Mariana was ready to leave.

"I'll do it," Mariana said, as Deirdre counted out her share of the money for the readings. "I'll try asking for a dream. But I want to do something else, too. I want to drive by Eric Cullen's shop and see if I can pick anything up from the energy there."

"You think you'll catch him making a bomb?" Deirdre handed Mariana the money and closed the cash register.

"No. I just want to see what the place feels like. Mind if I borrow the telephone directory? I need an address."

Mariana found the address, only because Eric Cullen had been considerate enough to list himself as owner of Top of the Line Body Shop in the Yellow Pages ad. The shop was on Thompson, in midtown Ventura, one of a number of auto repair shops in a cluster not too far from where she lived.

"Don't go in," Deirdre said.

"I'll just drive by," Mariana replied. "Although the Mustang could use a paint job."

"Call me when you get home."

Mariana shook her head, not wanting to be fussed over, and left the store.

She took the short drive to Thompson and slowed down when she reached the block, looking for a sign so that she could tell which of the small repair shops was the right one.

Top of the Line Body Shop had an address on Thompson, but was actually set back from the street, almost all the way to Front Street, the last street before the railroad tracks, the freeway, Harbor Boulevard, and the beach. Mariana decided to drive around the block to get a better look.

But there was really nothing to see. A narrow asphalt parking area with more cars than parking spaces and a garage with three racks, all of them in use. A small office. That was it.

There were five men working on the cars, all wearing dirty gray uniforms. Mariana wondered which one was Eric Cullen. She decided he had to be the big man with blond, curly hair. He seemed to be in charge.

Deirdre was right, of course. Mariana wasn't likely to catch him working on a bomb. Especially at six in the evening, with the sun still up. The thing to do was to drive by later, see if he really worked until ten.

Mariana drove home, fed the cats, fed herself, and found that she couldn't settle into her regular evening routine, tired as she was. She wanted to know what Eric Cullen was doing.

She forced herself to wait until nine o'clock before she left the house. She wrapped herself in a shawl, not because she needed protection from the elements, but because it brought her comfort.

The evening air was a comfortable sixty-five degrees, practically a year-round norm in Ventura. For about ten months of the year, the temperature rose to a high of seventy during the day and dropped to a low of fifty at night. Not much summer, but not much winter, either. Mariana couldn't complain about the cold. Still, the shawl felt good.

The short trip down Thompson didn't quite confirm Eric Cullen's alibi, but it confirmed that he might have had one. The lights were out at the four other shops that were part of the same cluster. Not at Top of the Line. Three men were still working on what appeared to be a dark blue Jaguar, and one of the men was the big blond.

Mariana couldn't think of a good reason to talk to them, so she slowly drove home again.

Deirdre was right. The only thing she could do was ask for a dream of Jeannie.

The dream came toward morning, and Mariana struggled to hold on to the images when she woke up.

She had been standing in a meadow, and Jeannie had waved to her from the other side of the stream—a transformed Jeannie, smiling, glad to see her. Then she and Jeannie were flying, hand in hand, through the night sky. The ocean was below them. Then they were over a building of some kind—Mariana couldn't quite make it out—and Jeannie wanted to take her inside, but then they were both afraid. Jeannie vanished, and Mariana woke up.

That was all.

A dream of Jeannie. *Borne like an angel on the summer air.* Except that in the song Jeannie was borne like a vapor, not an angel. Nothing was quite right.

The building. Was there a way of finding the building?

Was it even in Ventura? It didn't look like a house, more like an office building, but the image had been hazy.

Mariana hurried to get ready to go to Enchantment, eager to compare dreams with Deirdre.

But Deirdre was busy with customers, and Mariana had two clients waiting, and it was the middle of the afternoon before Mariana could tell Deirdre about her trip to the body shop, and before they had a chance to compare dreams.

"Well, Jeannie certainly wants to communicate with you," Deirdre said, when Mariana had told her dream. "And your dream was more helpful than mine. All I got was the image of Jeannie lying dead on the floor while two men with gloves on messed up the living room. Neither one was a big blond."

"If you saw them, though, maybe you could pick them out of a book," Mariana said. "Mug shots."

"No. All I could tell was that they were both more brownish than blondish. They had baseball caps on, and facial hair, and jackets pulled up high. I don't think Jeannie knew them."

Mariana sighed. "David told me when we first met that psychic information was always interesting, usually right, and never helped him solve a case. I'd really like to prove him wrong."

"We have a start," Deirdre said. "We know we have to find a building near the beach."

"We?" Mariana had expected Deirdre to try to talk her out of looking for the building.

"Well, you. I have to be home to take care of the kids tonight."

"And I'm having dinner with David."

"Then after dinner you can take a nice, romantic drive along the beach and look for that building."

"I'll think about it. I'm not sure David would agree."

They were interrupted by Mariana's third client, who turned out to be her last for the afternoon. Because it was slow, Mariana checked out a little early. And because it was Saturday, she wouldn't be seeing Deirdre for the next four days.

"Call me tomorrow," Deirdre said, as Mariana prepared to leave. "Don't make me wait until Thursday to find out about your date. Or about the building, either."

"I'll call if there's anything to tell. And call me if you get another dream."

Mariana stepped out into a late afternoon that was a little sunnier than the preceding days. She still felt a chill.

By the time she had gone home, fed the cats, and put on a little fresh makeup, the chill had settled into her bones. She wished she hadn't made the date with David.

Just before seven, she heard his footsteps on the stairs.

"I'm early," he said as she opened the door.

"It's all right. I'm ready."

They walked down the stairs in silence, not speaking until they were both settled into his car.

"I thought we might go to that café on Thompson," David said, starting the engine.

"That's fine. We could drive by Eric Cullen's shop on the way, see if he's working late," Mariana replied.

David frowned. His gray moustache twitched before he answered. "If there's something you have to tell me about Jean Cullen's murder, let's get it over with before we have dinner."

"I'm not sure I have anything that will help, but Deirdre and I have both been dreaming of Jeannie."

"Okay, tell me." David turned off the engine. He leaned back in the seat and looked at her, waiting.

Mariana couldn't quite see his eyes. She wished she could see his eyes.

"Jeannie says it was two men, brownish complexion, facial hair, wearing jackets and baseball caps. She didn't know them. She thinks there was some kind of trade, that they murdered her because her husband is going to do something for someone else. There is a building involved, and I think it's near the beach. Maybe he's going to blow it up." She got it all out in one breath.

"All this from a dream," David said.

She still couldn't see his expression.

"From three dreams, actually—two of Deirdre's and one of mine."

"Anything else?"

"No." Mariana hesitated, then plunged on. "Except I was wondering if you had come up with any motives, either a motive for the burglary—something important stolen from the house—or a motive for murder."

"Nothing we could take to court. Cullen lost his wife at a convenient time. He's in debt, and the insurance money will get him out. And we heard he has a girl friend. On top of that, nothing of value was stolen from the house." David reached over and put his hand on her shoulder. "I'm telling you this because I'm treating you as part of the investigation on this case. I want to know anything either one of you picks up. Okay?"

"Does that mean we can take a drive along the beach and look for the building?"

"After dinner. But only if you promise to talk about something else from now until then."

Mariana promised. So over dinner and wine at the small café on Thompson they had one of those conversations that people have when they are avoiding talking about anything important, complete with awkward silences.

She was glad when it was over.

And he kept his promise.

"Which way?" he asked, when he had steered the car to Harbor Boulevard. He hadn't driven past Eric Cullen's shop on the way to dinner, but he did then. The lights were out, and he didn't slow down.

"I don't know. Let's try right. I think it's toward Santa Barbara, not Oxnard."

"In that case, I should have stayed on Thompson. Do you want me to pick up the freeway?"

"Yes."

It would have been a pleasant drive under other circumstances, with a full moon and a clear sky and the gentle waves breaking against the sand. But this wasn't going to work, and Mariana knew it almost at once.

"You might as well take me home," she said, even before they reached the Seacliff exit.

"Okay."

She could feel his disappointment. Until then, she hadn't realized that he wanted her to be right. There was something comforting about him wanting her to be right.

"I'm not going to ask you in," she said when he stopped the car in front of her door. Even though they weren't in the black-and-white, David accepted it as his prerogative as a police detective to park in a no-parking zone.

"I know." He leaned over and kissed her cheek. "Good-night."

Mariana was halfway up the stairs, and David had already driven away, when it hit her. Nothing about this was quite right. They should have turned left on Harbor Boulevard.

She wasn't certain what to do, whether to go in and try

to call him back, or to look for the building herself. But then a wave of urgency hit her. She had to look for the building. Now.

She walked back down to the carport, got in her car, and headed back to Harbor Boulevard, this time turning left.

When she saw the building, she recognized it at once, and wondered why she hadn't known it in the dream. It was a small, exclusive hotel, with an equally small and exclusive restaurant, a low rectangular building, dimly lit, right on the beach. And a dark blue classic Jaguar was parked in front of the restaurant.

The wave of urgency hit her again. It was quickly replaced by fear, the same fear that she had felt in the dream.

Mariana pulled over to the curb and jumped out of her car. She started running toward the restaurant, shouting as she ran.

"There's a bomb in the Jaguar! A bomb!"

She saw a door open, and a face appear.

"A bomb!" she cried again. "In the car! Run!"

People began streaming out of the restaurant, customers and staff, running away from the building.

But when the explosion came, it wasn't from the car. The entire restaurant turned into a fireball before her eyes.

Mariana stood, too stunned to say anything when a security guard appeared beside her and twisted her arm up behind her back.

"Let's sit down, right where we are, and wait for the police," he said.

Mariana nodded. That was exactly what she wanted to do.

The firefighters were the first to arrive, followed closely by three police cars. She sat locked in the back of a black-and-white until David arrived to take her home for the second time that evening.

Mariana didn't call Deirdre on Sunday. She spent much of the day recovering from the fear and the shock of the night before, a recovery made only a little easier by the sense that the spirit of Jeannie Cullen was hovering over her bed, wanting her to be all right.

Deirdre had been watching television news, though, and she left two messages that Mariana ignored. Deirdre knew she was all right. The details would have to wait until she felt like sharing them.

Only after David had called on Monday to fill in the missing pieces did Mariana pick up the phone and call Enchantment.

"The bomb target was Senator Fordham," Mariana said. "She and her husband occasionally use that particular hotel for a weekend getaway. Several people knew they would be there this weekend. And everybody knows they enjoy late dinners. Nobody raised an eyebrow when a well-dressed blond man with a briefcase parked a Jaguar out front and asked for a table. Nobody noticed when he went to the men's room and didn't come back."

"So they have Eric Cullen for the bombing, if not his wife's murder. Does David know who the co-conspirator is yet?" Deirdre asked.

"The FBI is swarming all over the case, but the rumor is that someone wanted to remove the one strong anti-war voice from the Armed Services Committee," Mariana told her. "It centers around the shop. I'm almost certain that one of Cullen's employees is the link. But I've been not-quite-right on so much, starting with my dream of an earthquake. It felt like an earthquake, but it was an explosion. I think I would have responded differently from the beginning if I had dreamed of an explosion."

"But you still succeeded in saving all those people. Is David ready to admit that he was wrong? That psychics can help solve a case?"

"He was even cheerful about it."

"So are you seeing him tonight?" Deirdre sounded like a teenager, and Mariana didn't feel like giggling with her. Not yet.

"Tonight I'm asking for a dream of Jeannie," Mariana said. "It's time to get it right, time to say thank you, and goodbye."

Too Many Cooks

A Freddie O'Neal Mystery

Freddie O'Neal and a story with a recipe? I wasn't sure how I was going to handle that combination when I received an invitation to write a story for Murder Most Delicious, *but then I realized that it didn't have to be her recipe. Somebody else could be the cook.*

"You're not what I expected, and I'm not sure this is going to work."

I could have said the same to her. The woman who had called to make an appointment, and who was now standing at the front door to my house—which doubles as my office door was Belinda Blackburn, star of "Barbecue with Belinda," a Saturday morning ratings hit on the Public Access TV channel. I had never watched her show, since I limit my cooking to lifting the corner on a frozen dinner and sticking it in the microwave, but I had seen her picture on posters at the supermarket that sponsored the program. The photos had led me to expect a cheerful woman in her late thirties, with short, dark, flyaway hair, and maybe a little bit of a weight problem.

In person, Belinda Blackburn did have short, dark, flyaway hair, although a little gray showed. But she was closer to fifty than forty, and nobody that well-tailored would consider weight a problem. Her beige suit must have had some kind of designer label, or it would never have fit both the thin shoulders and the sloping breasts. Where the picture had clearly lied, however, was in the impression of cheer. Her round face, adorned with so much makeup that it seemed permanently camera-ready, was drawn with worry. A furrow between her eyes ran straight into a too-narrow nose. Red lipstick had crept into the lines above her lips, which were pressed tightly together.

"Do you want to come in or forget it?" I asked.

"Unfortunately, I don't think I have a choice," she replied. "I inquired, and you are the only woman in Reno licensed as a private investigator. So yes, thank you, I will come in."

I graciously ushered her to one of the two folding chairs sitting in front of my desk and took my spot in the big leather chair behind it. I had straightened up after she called, but I spied a glob of gray cat fur that I had missed, neatly swept it up, and dropped it in the wastebasket.

"Why do you need a private investigator?" We could get to the "woman" question later.

"Someone is sabotaging my show."

She waited for a reaction, but I couldn't come up with the appropriate outrage.

"What makes you think that?"

"Things happen. Once the refrigerator was set to defrost, so the molded salad didn't gel. Another time, the plug I use for the electric charcoal starter was shorted out, so the coals weren't ready. Two weeks ago, someone substituted turpentine for the white vinegar. Fortunately, I sniffed before I poured." She thunked her handbag onto the desk for emphasis.

"You do your show live, right? Isn't that the kind of thing that always happens on live television?"

"I was ready to believe that. But last week I was doing a show featuring game, and when I lifted the lid off the marinade, on camera, a dead rabbit was lying there. And not the rabbit the supermarket had provided. This one had fur, ears, and a tail."

"That must have been upsetting," I admitted, "and it doesn't sound like an accident."

"No-o-o-o-o," she said, drawing it out as though I were a child. "And that's why I need a private investigator. I want to know who is doing this."

"The series of incidents, especially the dead rabbit, sounds like you could make a case for harassment. You could go to the police."

"I could." She nodded, pleased with me. "I could make a report. And the report would be filed, and they might send someone out to question the people who work with me, and they would add that report to the file. And I wouldn't know who was doing it, and they couldn't catch the person that way."

"So what do you want from me?"

"I want to hire you as my assistant. Undercover. That way you'll have a reason to be on the set. You can catch whoever it is in the act and make a citizen's arrest. That's why I needed a woman. I needed someone who could be a credible assistant, who knew her way around a kitchen." She smiled expectantly, looking for an instant almost like the "Barbecue with Belinda" ads.

"Would you like a cup of coffee?" I asked.

"Why, yes, thank you. If it's made—I don't want you to make a pot just for me."

"I don't own a pot."

The furrow reappeared.

"I make coffee by sticking a cup of tap water in the microwave and adding instant when bubbles appear," I continued.

Her jaw dropped, and she struggled to pull it back.

"I understand what you're telling me," she said. "So we have to think of another way to make this work. What skills do you have?"

My jaw dropped on that one.

"I'm good at what I do, but I'm not sure how to describe it in terms of skills," I said. "I've never thought of it that way."

She looked around the office. There wasn't much to see except desk, computer, bookcases, and my Union Pacific poster.

"Do you type?" she asked. "Can you use a word processor?"

I nodded warily.

"Fine," she said. "You're going to help me with a book. Come to my house tomorrow morning at nine, and we'll work out the details. The meeting to plan this week's show starts at eleven, and I can introduce you to everyone then."

"Is this a ritual?"

"Yes. We finalize the menu on Thursday, prepare everything on Friday, and tape on Saturday. Every week." She appraised me one more time. "I don't suppose I could ask you to wear a skirt."

"I'll be there at eleven. In jeans. We can talk after the meeting."

She pondered that for a moment, then nodded.

"Do you want a check now?" she asked.

"Yes, thank you, I do."

Suddenly I found myself prepared to like her after all.

After the requisite piece of paper changed hands, she left. I sat there, trying to think of someone I could call to get information about the show, and decided I would have to go to the supermarket. That was as good a place to start as any. I was about to walk out the door when the phone rang.

"I thought you might want to come for dinner Saturday night," Mom said. "It's Al's birthday, and I'm inviting a few friends."

"Al will be happier if I'm not one of them. I don't think he considers me a friend."

Mom had married Al when I was sixteen, and our relationship had never progressed beyond tense.

"But he does consider you family, and it is his birthday." She said it in her cooing tone, which meant she really did want me to come. "Besides, we just got a new barbecue, and Al is having such a good time with it. He really wants to try some of the recipes for a crowd."

"Barbecue? Al barbecues?"

"Yes. He decided that if Belinda Blackburn does it, anyone could."

"Do you watch her show?"

"Not really, but Al does. I've never been able to get interested in cooking."

"I know." I said it as flatly as I could.

"That's one of the mistakes I made with you, isn't it?" She was off and running. I could hear it in her voice. "I was exposed to cooking when I was young, and I decided it wasn't something I wanted to do. But I didn't expose you to it when you were a child, and so you weren't able to make an educated decision about it. Especially since by the time you reached seventh grade, girls weren't required to take Home Ec anymore, so you took woodworking instead."

"It's okay, Mom, I don't build bookshelves, either."

"No, but at least you had the opportunity. And it isn't too late, you know. You could still take a cooking class. You might like it. An aversion to steam rising from a soup pot isn't in the genes."

"I'll think about it. What can you tell me about 'Barbecue with Belinda'?"

"It's a stupid show, but Al likes it."

I bit my tongue, and she continued.

"Belinda Blackburn, who might look all right on television if she lost forty pounds and got her hair done, pretends every Saturday morning that two dozen people just dropped by for barbecue, and she just happens to have enough bread, salad, dessert, and fresh road kill in the refrigerator to pull it off. With, naturally, the proper wine for each course."

"The supermarket poster says she shoots it live. Do people actually eat on camera?"

"Oh, yes. Someone always passes little tidbits for her so-called guests to share. Why do you care?"

"I don't know. I was sort of thinking about getting a barbecue." Professional privilege stopped me from telling her the truth.

"Then you must come Saturday night," she said triumphantly. "You and Al will have something in common."

"For the first time," she might have added, but didn't.

"Okay. I'll be there." Agreeing was easier than arguing, and I could always leave early. Al wouldn't mind.

I still had to go to the supermarket, because I had to feed two cats who had decided long ago that foraging was better than eating dried food, and I was out of canned. A trip to the supermarket was less work than scrubbing sparrow blood off the carpet.

The cashier at the supermarket didn't watch the show, so I decided I could play it by ear. Early—for me—the next morning, I hopped in the Jeep and drove to Belinda Blackburn's house.

Belinda Blackburn lived in the old money section of town, the part of California Street on the hill overlooking Reno High School. Even though I was there only a few minutes past eleven, the circular driveway was already full of cars. I parked at the curb, under something old and deciduous. A few falling leaves wouldn't hurt the Jeep. The owners of the Cadillac, the Plymouth, and the two Hondas in the driveway were probably more careful. And especially the owner of the '68 Mustang. That stopped me for a moment. I used to own a restored '68 Mustang, and this one was cherry.

A kid in his late teens, twenty tops, opened the door when I rang. He was a thin version of Belinda, in ragged Levi's and a UNR t-shirt, with sparkling eyes and bad skin.

"Are you Mom's new assistant?" he asked.

"How'd you know?"

"She said to look for a woman with no makeup, long blond hair, and jeans. You're the only one today."

"You've got me. I'm Freddie O'Neal."

I held out my hand.

"I'm Will Blackburn," he said, shaking it. "They're all in back, on the set."

"The set is here?"

"Yeah. It costs more to shoot it here than at the studio, but Mom wanted control, and she figured this was the best way to get it. Follow me."

He led me across the living room—I got a glimpse of fresh flowers and lime-green brocade—and through open French doors to a wide brick veranda. From there we could see the set. Belinda Blackburn was standing with three other people in front of a barbecue big enough for a Brahma bull. A refrigerator was improbably close, framed by a grape trellis, and a long picnic table sat where the orchestra pit should be, with enough concrete around it for two large cameras. A track several feet above the table held still another camera.

Belinda was arguing with three people who were each younger than she was, but that seemed to be their only advantage.

"Not bear," a woman wearing glasses and carrying a notebook was saying. "I don't care if the Indians ate it, I don't care if Davy Crockett loved the taste, no one is going to come into the store on Saturday morning and ask for bear steak. I guarantee it."

"What do you suggest then?" The frost in Belinda's voice would have made a strong man long for a blanket.

"Chicken," she pleaded. "Chicken's always good."

"*Chicken!* I've done chicken. Everyone's done chicken." Belinda paused for effect and smiled, sort of. "I want to do bear. And if you won't provide it, I'll find someone who will."

I wasn't sure whether I wanted to leap into that group. Staying on the veranda seemed safer.

"Okay," I said to Will. "That one's the supermarket rep. Who are the other two?"

"The woman in the straw hat is the production manager, and the guy is Mom's gofer," he replied.

"Does she really want to barbecue a bear?"

"It's hard to tell. Sometimes she asks for weird things just so another request sounds reasonable."

"Got it. Thanks." I stepped onto the artistically broken

concrete path to the set, and then turned back. "Hey. Is the Mustang yours?"

Will Blackburn lit up like a Christmas tree.

"Yeah. She's my baby."

I nodded. I knew how he felt.

By the time I reached the group, someone had mentioned quail, and Belinda was considering the idea.

"All right, quail," she announced, and with barely time for breath she added, "Freddie O'Neal, I want you to meet Stella Chism, Bobby Archuletta, and Janice Turner."

"Pleased to meet you," I said. Each one murmured something polite.

"Freddie is helping me with a book, based on the show," Belinda said, with an amazing confidence that the story would be believed.

Janice Turner, the supermarket rep, looked surprised, but not unhappy with the idea. Stella Chism, the production manager, shrugged. Bobby Archuletta looked aghast.

"A book?" he whispered. "You're doing a book? And you didn't let me know?"

"I'm sorry, dear," Belinda said, patting him on the shoulder. "I meant to tell you before Freddie got here, but it slipped my mind."

"We could work something out to trade it for coupons, based on register receipts," Janice Turner said. "Not bad."

"What do you think of quail, Freddie?" Belinda asked.

"Kind of messy," was all I could come up with. In truth, I had never eaten one. But quail are common in Reno, and Butch and Sundance like them even better than sparrows.

"You're right." Belinda was pleased with me. She patted my shoulder this time. "All those tiny bones. But I think we can do it." She turned to the barbecue. "Just imagine all those tiny bodies, bursting with an olive oil and raspberry vinegar marinade, with just a touch of fresh rosemary, stretched across the coals."

"You got it, Belinda," Janice said, making a note.

"And watermelon," Belinda added. "Champagne-filled watermelon. Half a dozen should do it."

"What else?" Janice sighed, but it sounded as if this would be a deal.

"Herbed rice, grilled corn, sweet-and-sour cucumbers, and chocolate mousse," Belinda snapped.

"No. Not chocolate mousse." The words sprang from Bobby as if he had been holding them in for days. "I know you like chocolate mousse, Belinda, but God, no, not again. Besides, it's just too rich. Especially after champagne watermelon."

Belinda faltered.

"What then?" she asked.

"Cookies," Bobby pleaded. "The cookies will go with the watermelon and the coffee."

"All right." Belinda sighed. "But choose something delicate."

"Butter cookies, with a touch of Grand Marnier," Bobby insisted. "And we'll dip one side in chocolate."

"Wonderful!" Belinda gasped.

Bobby smiled, relieved.

"I'll work it out with Janice and Stella," he said.

The group started back to the house. Belinda stayed near the barbecue.

"What do you think?" she asked.

"Too soon to tell. I'll have to be here tomorrow, to watch the preparations, and then Saturday for the taping. How secure will the set be tomorrow night?"

"Very. I have a Rottweiler."

"Fine. Where is he now?"

"In the garage. But I let him have the run of the yard most of the time."

"Okay." That sounded secure enough to me. "When do you start cooking?"

"The food will arrive around ten, and we'll start immediately."

"I'll see you then."

I might have stayed a little longer, to maintain the fiction of a book in progress, but it didn't seem useful. I'd be spending enough time there in the next two days.

I said good-bye to Will, and good-bye to the Mustang as well. It was still there, waxed and gorgeous, when I got back the next morning, along with the Cadillac and the two Hondas. A supermarket delivery truck was just pulling away.

Will answered again when I rang.

"Are you sure you want to do this?" he asked.

"Is your mother's check any good?"

"I hope so. You're going to earn it."

He stepped back, and I could hear raised voices.

"Lead me to it," I said.

Belinda's kitchen looked as if she had handed a designer a picture from *Better Homes and Gardens* and told him to do it, damn the cost. It was bigger than my office, bedroom, and kitchen combined, with skylights and a butcher block working-area in the center, and about everything else a lover of culinary display could imagine.

Half a dozen watermelons, bright green with faint stripes, lay side by side on the butcher block. Stella Chism was waving a large knife over the first one, not certain where to plunge it in.

"The end!" Bobby was yelling. "The plug goes in the end! Otherwise you can't pour the champagne into glasses the next day."

"The top! Otherwise the champagne leaks during the night, and only half the watermelon is saturated!" Belinda replied in a tone that would have convinced me. "And if you carve it properly, you have a boat for fruit salad on Sunday!"

"Leftovers," Bobby moaned. "You're worried about left-overs. There aren't any leftovers from champagne water-melon. I don't care how many you're serving!"

"Three from the top, and three from the end," Stella said. "How's that?"

"This is my show!" Belinda roared. "The watermelons will be cut the way I say they will be cut!"

"You're right, Belinda," Bobby said meekly.

Stella waited, knife still poised.

"Stella, cut three plugs from the end, and three from the top. We'll start pouring champagne from the three with plugged ends, and we'll leave the other three, in case we want salad boats," Belinda ordered.

Stella nodded and began cutting plugs.

The same scene was repeated, with minor variations, as every item was prepared. Should the corn be cleaned and wrapped in foil or barbecued in its own husk? Should the sweet-and-sour cucumber have sugar or honey in the dressing? Should the herbed rice have oregano or what? What was the best ratio of olive oil to raspberry vinegar for the quail marinade? Belinda always won, although when Stella was able to come up with a Solomonic compromise, Belinda would take it.

Except for the cookies. Belinda didn't argue over the cookies. It was late afternoon by the time they got to the cookies, but Belinda didn't even have to tell Bobby he could do what he wanted with them. That evidently had been a prior arrangement.

The day had worn on without any formal breaks except for lunch, although coffee was available. Lunch had been kind of a disappointment. Bobby arranged some of the cucumber slices on white bread, after he cut the crusts off, laid a sprig of watercress diagonally on each, and cut up some carrots and celery ribs. He added small bunches of purple grapes. I couldn't understand how in the world Belinda had expected to pass me off as her assistant when she had Bobby, even though he didn't have the title.

The plates looked pretty, but I would rather have had the bread crusts, which Bobby tossed out. A lot of food is wasted on a cooking show. After lunch, I still wanted a hamburger.

Stella cleaned up the kitchen while Bobby dropped teaspoons of cookie dough on sheets of metal. Belinda motioned me out into the backyard.

"Well? What do you think?" she asked.

"I think if one of them is messing you up, it's not going to happen while I'm watching. We're going to have to see what goes wrong tomorrow, if anything, and I'll take it from there."

"I'm paying you to see that nothing goes wrong."

"You're paying me to do my best. If the Rottweiler does his, we should be all right."

Belinda pursed her lips and let me go.

I returned at the crack of dawn the next morning, or so it felt. But the worker bees were already hard at it. Stella, again in her straw hat, was giving instructions to the camera crew, and Bobby was carrying food from the kitchen to the picnic table, stopping every second trip to check the coals. Several clusters of folding chairs had been set up on the lawn, waiting for the "guests." Janice Turner was sitting in one, making notes. Belinda was nowhere to be seen, and

Will had disappeared after letting me in.

I wandered around, trying to watch everyone and stay out of the way at the same time. If I hadn't happened to stroll behind the refrigerator trellis, I never would have seen it. A watermelon was half-hidden by the grape leaves.

The area seemed deserted—all the activity was in front—but I decided not to touch the watermelon. I kept strolling. A chair cluster was close enough to the edge of the set that by pulling one chair a little farther to the side, I could see anybody who walked behind the trellis. I settled down to wait.

A few couples drifted in, the men mostly in polo shirts and slacks, the women mostly in blouses and skirts. I suspected Belinda had a dress code, and I was the only one violating it. Janice didn't leave her chair, Stella stayed with the cameras, and Bobby kept up a frantic pace between the kitchen and the picnic table. No one stepped behind the set.

Shortly before airtime, Belinda appeared, wearing a dark blue dress with a red-and-white apron that made her look like a flag. With Bobby at her side, the two of them checked out everything that had been prepared the day before. Everything but the watermelon behind the trellis.

When it came, the move was so subtle, so much a part of the action, that I almost missed it. Stella had started the countdown for the cameras, and all eyes were on Belinda. I sensed, more than saw, a blur at the corner of my vision.

Will Blackburn was sliding the watermelon from behind the trellis onto the picnic table, next to the others.

"All right!" I shouted. "What's in the watermelon?"

I jumped from the chair and reached the table in two steps, grabbing his arms.

His eyes were wide with fear, and his arms went slack.

The watermelon fell to the concrete, shattering like a skull. Something bright red that wasn't champagne splattered all over both of us.

"Kool-Aid!" he gasped. "It's just Kool-Aid!"

"Kool-Aid!" Belinda screamed. "It's supposed to be champagne!"

"There's champagne in the others, Mom, just not this one."

He was struggling to get loose, but I had him firmly.

"Why did you do it?" Belinda cried. Her eyes were as wide as her son's, an almost endearing family picture.

"Ratings," Will said, still gasping for breath. "That's why people watch the show—to see you cope with everything that goes wrong!"

Belinda was too stunned to speak, but her mouth kept moving. Suddenly, it formed a smile. She turned to the cameras, which had been running the whole time.

"I think we all need a glass of champagne after this," she said sweetly. "Will, why don't you start pouring?"

There was a chorus of cheers and laughter from the audience. Bobby and Will filled glasses from the unplugged watermelons, and I took one when they got to me, even though I don't normally drink that early in the day.

The rest of the show went without a hitch.

I waited until Belinda was free afterwards, even though I wanted to get out of my Kool-Aid stained clothes as soon as possible. They were sticky, and my skin was starting to itch.

"What do you want to do now?" I asked her.

"You did your job, and I can handle my son," she said.

"Don't be too tough on him."

Belinda shook her head. "Of course not. After all, he may be right."

I could have offered her some confirmation from the

messages on my answering machine when I got home. Mom put it the most succinctly.

"Al thought you were even better than the rabbit," she chortled. "Come for dinner, please."

I wasn't surprised when it turned out to be quail.

Barbecued Quail

Marinade:
½ cup olive oil
¼ cup raspberry vinegar
2 tablespoons chopped fresh rosemary
2 cloves garlic
Salt and pepper to taste

Clean and split quail, soak in marinade for at least one half hour, drain, then barbecue over fairly hot coals, five to eight minutes per side, basting frequently with reserved marinade. Game hen does well in this marinade, if you don't have quail, but needs about fifteen minutes per side over the coals. Duck also barbecues well, especially if you start it in the oven, drain off the fat, and then finish it on the barbecue. If you have a rosemary bush, add a branch to the coals before grilling the birds.

These are great cold for lunch the next day.

Billy the Goat

A Freddie O'Neal Mystery

The investment scam in this story is one that I had heard of some years earlier and had filed away for future use. When I decided the scam would involve Freddie's cousin, there had to be a motive stronger than simple greed. And what could that be but passion?

"What Cousin Billy? You mean the Cousin Billy who dragged me around Idlewild pool with my head under water when I was six years old? That Cousin Billy?"

"You only have one Cousin Billy, the son of your Aunt Freddie, for whom you were named. Yes. That Cousin Billy."

"She doesn't even send me birthday cards, and I wouldn't recognize either of them on the street. And Billy has to be fortysomething. Why would a fortysomething man still use the name Billy?"

"I don't know. You'll have to ask him."

"Why does he want to see me? And why doesn't he just call?"

"I can't answer either of those questions," Ramona snapped.

She was getting testy, probably because I was. Her relationships with her sister, her sister's assorted husbands, and her sister's three adult children weren't any better than mine. So it wasn't fair of me to push her.

On the other hand, it wasn't fair of Cousin Billy to call her after all these years and ask a favor. Especially when the favor he asked was to arrange a quiet meeting with me. Which meant my mother had to ask me a favor.

Not a good start for a telephone call.

"Okay." I figured I could give in on this one. Find out for myself what was going on with Billy. "Where are we supposed to meet?"

"The Arcade at the Clarion."

"The Arcade? You mean the place next to the ice cream counter where the video games are? The place where the kids are dropped while the adults gamble?"

"That way you can spot each other. He'll be playing Space Invaders, tonight at seven."

"He could be playing anything he likes. He'll be the only person over twelve."

"I think that was the idea. He wasn't certain he could recognize you, either."

"All right. I'll see what he wants."

"Thank you." Her tone was icy. Asking me to help a nephew she hadn't seen in twenty-five years was tough.

"And I'll call you tomorrow."

She hung up without thanking me again.

The Clarion wasn't one of my favorite places, but I could understand why Billy—or anyone else needing to set up a discreet meeting by way of a third party—might choose it. It was one of the newer hotel-casinos, built a couple of miles south of the downtown gambling center, and airport-handy. There were always at least three conventions on the daily schedule, and the crowd at the tables would welcome the space in a sardine can.

Two people could have a conversation without the possibility of being taped in the din. Only a lip reader would have a shot at picking it up.

I pulled the Jeep into the parking lot about fifteen minutes early. The asphalt covered an area the size of a football field. Even so, the first space I spotted was against the back fence.

The sun hadn't set, and the early evening air was still warm. By late May, the temperature swings run around forty degrees, dropping slowly from the mid-eighties in the afternoon to the low forties just before dawn. I figured this wouldn't take much time, so I hadn't bothered to bring a jacket.

I walked down a long row of cars, vans, and pickups, mostly with California plates. I wondered where Billy had been living for the past twenty-five years. Not in Reno, I was certain of that.

Scattered lines of people converged on the double doors from the parking lot to the casino, like ants discovering a chocolate bar.

The inside was a sudden explosion of light, color, and sound. Another football field, with the center open for a couple of stories straight up, the floor jammed with tables and machines all swarming with people.

A glass-encased announcement board welcomed the conventions of the day—orthopedic surgeons, travel writers, and the Arkansas Bar Association.

I stayed on the outskirts of the pit as much as possible, working my way toward the corner escalator that led to the hollowed-out second floor, where the video games and ice cream counter were located.

The post-World War II gamblers who built the city were probably rattling their dry bones in wonder at the new emphasis on family-friendly entertainment, and the way gambling had morphed from a pastime somewhere between sleazy and sinful to good, clean fun and a healthy source of state revenue to boot.

The video game players were all minors, as usual. A sole adult stood just outside the area, a man about five foot seven, with reddish-brown hair, as twitchy as a pedophile watching for security guards.

Ironically, I would have recognized Billy after all. With that small, tight mouth and pointed chin, he had to share Ramona's gene pool.

The cowboy boots gave him some needed height, but he didn't seem comfortable in them, and they didn't exactly coordinate with his blue suit, white shirt, and burgundy tie. And he was still four inches shorter than I when he walked up and held out his hand.

"My God, Freddie, it's good to see you."

The hand was a little sweaty. I was glad he hadn't tried to hug me.

"Hey, Billy," I replied. I was trying to reconcile this thin, nervous man with the teenager who had seemed so powerful when he dragged me around the pool.

"We could have met at the bar. I would have recognized you—you look just like your father."

I took my hand back.

"I'd just as soon talk over a beer," I said.

"Fine, fine. How about dinner? We need a little time to catch up."

"I can't handle the line at the buffet, but the area that serves the little pizzas would be okay."

"I was thinking about the restaurant across the way." He gestured to the area on the other side of the doughnut hole, where the exception to the rule that casinos serve inexpensive food hid behind a bright seafood menu and a dark door.

Billy had to be doing pretty well. Or be using someone else's credit card. It wasn't a nice thought, but the combination of the twitchiness and the reference to my father brought my guard up.

"Your choice," I said.

We walked the balcony in silence. Billy was working hard at the cowboy boots, but they were pitching him forward, and I was reminded of the way a baby walks, almost falling with every step, half-running just to stay upright.

Billy looked both ways quickly before slipping through the door.

A smiling man in a tux who stood somewhere between Billy's height and mine showed us to a corner booth in a room so dim that I couldn't tell if it was full or empty or somewhere in between. He handed us menus and left.

I set mine aside.

"You know what you want?" Billy asked.

"Catch of the Day and a beer," I said. "Now cut the crap and tell me what this is about."

"I thought we might chat a little first."

He looked hopeful, but I didn't help him out. He shook his head and sighed.

"I need you to run an errand for me." The hazel eyes tried to look sincere, but the lids twitched.

"What kind of errand? Why me?"

"I need someone I can trust, and someone who can take care of herself in a tight situation."

"Start from the beginning."

He couldn't focus. He waved at a waiter and ordered for both of us. I didn't bother to react.

"All right," Billy said, but he didn't sound as if he meant it. "I'm a stockbroker. I sell securities at a small, independent firm in Newport Beach—that's in Southern California. We do a lot of private placements for very wealthy people who want investments with an above average return. A few months ago a certain party approached me with an interesting idea—railroad tank cars."

"What's interesting about railroad tank cars?"

"These particular cars would be used to transport oil to Southern California. And they wouldn't be ordinary tank cars. These would be Cadillacs, not Chevys. With shining brass fixtures, and brass plates with the owner's name on the side. For a mere one hundred thousand dollars, a far-sighted individual could own a vehicle making continual trips from the oil-rich territories of Alaska to the automobile-dependent territories of Southern California. A can't-lose proposition."

He pulled a folded brochure from his inside coat pocket and flipped it open to a photograph of a tank car. The brass fixtures glowed, even in the imitation candlelight.

"This isn't a real tank car. This is a model," I said.

"Right. Every investor got a model of a tank car, just like the real one, as a desk ornament. Terrific sales tool."

"So what went wrong?"

Billy sighed. "Nothing was wrong with the idea. I did all the due diligence anyone could ask. The SEC approved the prospectus."

"So what went wrong?" I asked again.

"It seems the persons who wrote the prospectus and the persons who created the brochure took the word of the same party who talked to me. That is, we all believed that the tank cars were lined up."

"Whereas?"

"There are no tank cars." Billy cringed as he said it, waiting to be hit.

I shrugged. "You didn't create the scam. You didn't even write the prospectus. Turn the certain party in to the SEC. There might even be a reward."

"That seems like good advice." Billy was twitching again. He must twitch off about eight hundred calories a day. "But the certain party wouldn't like that at all. I need to keep a low profile. Getting in touch with the SEC would mean drawing a little too much attention. I'm not sure who I can trust—except you."

"Why me? You haven't seen me in twenty-five years."

"Hey, Freddie, you're my cousin. Who can you trust if you can't trust your cousin?"

Somebody who doesn't twitch, was what I thought.

"There's something you haven't told me," I said. "Like who this certain party is, the one behind the scam."

"I don't like the word 'scam.' I'd rather call it a misunderstanding." He looked around, making certain no one was within earshot, then lowered his voice anyway. "And I can't tell you the name of the party who put it together. You don't need to know. That isn't the problem here."

"If you say so. But then the problem has to be one of the guys who bought a tank car on your say-so."

"Right." Billy's eyes were starting to water. He reached up and rubbed them. "For whatever it's worth, there is only one. He's threatening to go to the SEC. And since I can't hand over the party behind the misunderstanding, a complaint means that I lose my license to sell securities, my livelihood."

"Are you the only broker selling these cars?"

"Not quite. Almost. There are three of us."

"But there's a prospectus. The other party's name has to be on it."

"I'm afraid it isn't."

"Oh, Billy." I shook my head. "You're not telling me your name is on the prospectus."

"And the other two brokers," he said. "It's not just me. It's like a limited partnership with a silent partner."

"That has to be illegal."

Billy didn't answer. He shifted in his chair and rubbed his eyes again.

The waiter brought my beer, Billy's martini, and a basket of rolls.

"Dinner will be right up," he said cheerfully.

"Looking forward to it," Billy said, with what he surely hoped was a believable smile.

"How did the silent partner talk you three supposedly astute financial types into risking your licenses and livelihoods like this?"

The rolls were sourdough, and warm. I tore one apart and buttered it while Billy decided what he was going to tell me.

"By explaining why it was better that the SEC think it was a deal put together by three Southern California stockbrokers and by pointing out how much more lucrative it was for us. We'd be getting not just the sales commissions, but a cut of the partnership profits as well."

"Greed. The silent partner appealed to your greed."

"In a word." Billy nodded, doing his best to hold on to the smile. "And what's wrong with greed? Every man pursuing his own self-interest is what makes the invisible hand of the marketplace work."

"Or not. If every man pursues his own self-interest at the expense of every other man, and woman, the marketplace is a jungle, and no invisible hand can turn it into a civilization. That takes effort and goodwill."

"Have it your way. I didn't come here to argue with you."

"That's right. You came to ask me a favor."

"Jesus. You're not making this easy."

"What do you want me to do, Billy?"

"I just want you to talk to the guy. He's staying at the hotel, with the orthopedic surgeons' group. Ask him to forget about the SEC. Tell him I'll give him back the money. Out of my own pocket. Please."

"You also want me to tell him you're sorry? And you'll never do it again?"

"Whatever it takes to get him off my back."

"Why can't you take the elevator to his room and tell him yourself?"

"I tried to tell him myself. He said he'd hurt me if he saw me again. And the other party might hurt me, too."

Billy shrank in his chair as he said it. I wondered how big this surgeon was. And how big the silent partner was.

"I'll have to think about it."

"Sure. We'll eat first." He took a deep breath. "And talk about something else. How's your mother?"

"Fine. You ought to go up to the lake and see her while you're in the area. Do you have a car?"

"Yeah. A blue Acura. And the rental agency gave me a map to go with it. Maybe I'll drive up there tomorrow."

"I'm sure she'd like that."

"How are you? You ever get married?"

"No. You?"

"Yeah, twice. One kid from the first. I guess I should have sent you an announcement or something."

Billy shifted in his chair again.

It turned out to be a long dinner. The more we tried to talk, the less we had to say.

In the back of my mind, I was working out how to tell him I wouldn't do it. I didn't want to be anywhere near his scam, even to help him out from under a federal investigation.

But things about him—the shape and color of his eyes, the small hands with the long, narrow fingers, the way he separated his salmon steak from the tiny center bones—kept reminding me of Ramona. Saying no to him would be like saying no to her, only worse. I'd have to tell her about it afterward. And even though she wasn't close to her sister, she felt some kind of an undefined obligation, one she would expect me to honor.

All conversation had stopped by the time the waiter brought coffee.

Billy looked at me with desperate hope in his eyes, eyes that needed only mascara, liner, and three shades of eyeshadow to match Ramona's.

"How did you find out the tank cars weren't there?" I asked, still not ready to commit.

"The guy—the orthopedic surgeon—found out. The base of operations was supposed to be the railroad yard in Sparks. Since he was coming to Reno for the convention, he thought he'd drive three miles east to check out his investment. But nobody in Sparks had ever heard of the deal, so he called me. I made a few phone calls and discovered he was right. I flew up here yesterday, just to make sure there was no mistake."

"What did the silent partner have to say?"

"Oh, hell, the usual. That I jumped the gun. That the cars weren't supposed to start rolling until September first, and everything would be worked out by then."

"But?"

Billy shook his head. He took a sip of coffee before he answered. "But this is almost June, and we've started selling cars, and the prospectus—with my name on it—says they're already sitting in the yard. And even if there's some way everything will be different in September, I don't think the surgeon would be willing to wait. And I can't blame him. So I want to give him the money back."

"You have the check?"

"I wish I did." He reached into his jacket.

"Sorry for the delay, sir." The waiter slipped a black leather folder onto the table.

Billy froze, hand in his pocket.

"No problem," he whispered.

The waiter disappeared into the shadows.

"I have a down payment," Billy finished, his voice barely audible. He pulled out his wallet. "Ten now, the other ninety when I can get it together."

His hand was shaking as he held out a sealed envelope.

"Please."

I took the envelope. There was no name or any other mark on it.

"Where do I deliver it?"

"Upstairs. Room 1103. Theo Georgopoulos. And I owe you one, Freddie, I swear, if you ever need anything I can give."

I hoped it wouldn't come to that.

"Are you certain he's in his room?"

"No. But you might as well give it a shot while you're here."

"Okay. Where will you be?"

His eyebrows shot up, and his mouth formed a circle of speechless wonder.

"I have to report back to you," I said. "Let you know what happens. Where will you be?"

"How about the lounge? There's some kind of musical entertainment going on. I'll try for a table at the back."

"Okay. And thanks for dinner."

I left him there. I figured he could settle the bill without me.

Outside the black door, back in the light and noise, I had to reorient myself to find the elevators.

One stopped for me almost immediately. I rode alone to the eleventh floor.

Room 1103 was the second door on the right. Whoever had last gone in or out hadn't bothered to pull it quite shut. I knocked, and it moved.

"Dr. Georgopoulos?"

No answer.

I pushed with my elbow, and the door swung open.

A closet and bathroom blocked the sightline to the bed, beyond them on the left. A solid wall stopped the door on the right.

"Dr. Georgopoulos?"

I stepped cautiously over the threshold and moved just far enough forward to see the rest of the room.

A man was lying on the bed, legs partially hanging over the end.

He was wearing a dark suit, white shirt, and striped tie, almost an echo of Billy's outfit, both of them too formal for Reno. And he was here for a convention. Maybe he had decided to come back to his room and take a nap after some kind of formal presentation. He had unfastened his belt buckle and his pants, getting comfortable. Certainly he was big enough to intimidate someone as small as Billy. Probably six-foot-four, if he had been standing.

But he wasn't going to do that again.

His hair had receded to a fringe of black around a high, white dome. A bullet hole sat like a third eye in the center of his forehead.

The wall behind the bed was spattered with blood, as if the guy had been upright, and the shot had knocked him more or less onto the bed. The blood still looked runny, as if it might be fairly fresh.

I thought I heard a noise from the bathroom. A surge of adrenaline almost sent me flying back out of the room and into the hall, but I took a couple of deep breaths to get the fear and the anger under control, and realized the noise came from the room next door.

I had two choices. I could call hotel security and be stuck for an hour, or I could find Billy and make sure I hadn't been set up. If the guy hadn't been so obviously dead, or if I thought the perp had been hiding in the closet, I would have called security. As it was, I wanted to find Billy.

I slipped back to the door.

A man and woman were walking toward the elevator bank, arguing.

I listened for the elevator doors to open and close, the silence to return.

When I was certain the hall was clear, I left the room and turned away from the elevators. I found the stairs, walked down two flights, and decided I could ride the rest of the way.

I hoped Billy would be in the lounge. I really wanted Billy to be in the lounge.

I wish I could say I was surprised when he wasn't there.

He'd had more than enough time to settle the bill, stop in the men's room, and get to the lounge. I cleared a path through the crowd with my elbows and my boots, apologizing all the way, knowing I was too late to catch him in the parking lot if he wanted to escape that way.

Once out of the building, I picked up speed. I trotted to

the exit lane, then took it across the middle of the lot, checking the rows both ways for a little man in a blue Acura trying to head for the hills.

I couldn't spot Billy, and I wasn't ready to check the lot car by car, especially when I didn't have a license plate number.

On the off chance that he'd asked me to meet him at the hotel where he was staying, I went back inside and picked up the house phone near the door.

"Billy Davis's room. William Davis," I corrected.

"Just a minute," the operator answered.

The phone started ringing.

I let it ring until she came back on the line.

"He doesn't seem to be there. Would you like to leave a message?"

"Not just now."

If he had a room, he'd have to go back to it, sooner or later. I just had to find it. I thought again about telling security. I still wanted to talk to Billy first.

I had to check the lounge one more time.

On stage, a man with shoe-polish black hair and a face dripping with flop sweat was belting, "What's New, Pussycat," while the band behind him did its collective best to keep playing, and to keep him from keeling over in embarrassment.

Billy still wasn't at a table.

I looked around for a sign that would direct me to a restroom. A stall seemed to be as good a place as any to see what was in the envelope. All I saw were bright, Disneyesque parrots pointing me toward the buffet. I figured restrooms would be close to the buffet line, and I was at least right on that.

The restroom wasn't crowded. The first lucky thing that

had happened since I arrived at the casino.

The envelope contained just what Billy told me—his personal check for ten thousand dollars, made out to Theodore Georgopoulos.

For the first time, I wondered if something had happened to Billy after I left the restaurant, something that kept him from the lounge. I had to check out his room.

Finding his room would have been a lot easier in pre-electronic days, when rooms had keys instead of programmable cards, and messages were stuck in racks of key boxes behind the registration desk. I could have left him a message and watched where it was placed. But not here.

My only quick idea was the maître d' at the restaurant. If he wasn't bribable, or if Billy hadn't charged dinner to his room, I'd be reduced to calling security.

I retraced my steps to the escalator, rode to the second floor, then walked around the balcony to the dark restaurant door.

The maître d' smiled when he saw me.

"Did you forget something?" he asked.

"Not exactly. I wanted to split the dinner bill with my cousin, Billy Davis, and he's being stubborn. Could you possibly retrieve our check from the waiter and let me see it?" I had a twenty folded in my hand.

"Certainly," the maître d' said, still smiling, once the twenty was his.

He slipped into the dim recesses of the restaurant and came back with Billy's signed receipt. And I had the room number. Room 1115, right down the hall from the corpse.

I thanked the maitre d' and left the restaurant for the second time, heading again for the elevator bank and the eleventh floor.

I barely glanced at 1103 as I passed. The door was still

ajar. I hadn't pulled it shut, both because I wanted to leave it as I found it and because I didn't want to put my hands on anything in the vicinity of the dead man.

When I reached the door to Billy's room, I knocked, out of habit, not really expecting an answer.

But I could have sworn I heard a groan.

I knocked again.

"Billy? Are you there?"

Silence.

"Billy, if you're there, open up. Because if I leave, I'm coming back with hotel security. Two of them. One for the room down the hall, and one for you."

I was about to walk away when I heard someone turn the lock.

The woman who opened the door was easily six-foot-two in her stiletto heels. Long black hair hung straight down over her bare shoulders, all the way to her lace-trimmed red corset, the kind with matching underpants, and garters to hold up black fishnet stockings. Her arms were fleshy, and a roll of fat billowed softly over the satin-covered wires.

But the set of her wine-red mouth was hard. I glanced down at her hand, expecting a whip.

She was holding a gun.

"Come in," she said, blinking a heavy fringe of fake eyelashes. "You must be Billy's cousin. He's told me so much about you."

"Oh, God. Next you'll tell me he couldn't come to the door himself because he's tied up."

In bare feet we would have been eye to eye. I didn't like having to look up to meet her gaze.

She smiled one of those wide-lipped smiles that vampires use to expose their fangs.

"I'm going to step back from the door," she said.

"You're going to come in and shut it behind you. If you leave instead, I'm going to end your cousin's life and disappear before you can return with help. Do you understand?"

"Yes, ma'am."

She kept the gun on me as she moved away from the door. I followed her into a room that was the twin of 1103, except that the man on the bed was Billy, and he was still alive.

He was naked and gagged, and his hands were cuffed behind his back, but he was still alive.

I could tell because he squirmed, and his face turned red. He looked even smaller and more pathetic naked than he had in the suit and boots.

"Sit down." The woman used her gun to point toward a chair on the far side of the room.

I did as told.

She leaned against the wall, regarding me thoughtfully.

"What happens next?" I asked, not wanting to give her too much time to think. "I can't believe you're going to walk out of here and leave us to call the cops."

"No. I hadn't expected you, and I'm afraid I'll have to improvise. In fact, I had specifically told Billy to leave the situation to me. Fortunately, I suspected that he was weak enough to panic. I've had friends keeping tabs on him. And when I saw him meet you, I knew what he was doing. I was about to punish him when you knocked."

"We haven't been introduced. I'm Freddie O'Neal, and you are—?" I broke off the question to wait for her answer.

"You don't need to know my name. You can call me Sada if you like."

"Sada. Are you by some other name known as a financial whiz?"

"I don't think you need to know that, either."

"Maybe not, but if you are, it would make sense out of why three Southern California stockbrokers chose to risk their licenses in a scam. Had to be something more than greed."

"A scam? Naughty Billy. I've told him not to use that word."

Billy squirmed some more, drawing his knees up to protect his genitals. He tried to make sounds through the gag.

"He called it a misunderstanding," I said.

Billy nodded rapidly.

"Good Billy," Sada purred.

Billy didn't relax his knees.

Sada looked at me again.

"I had hoped I could control Billy, at least until the money from investors was safely deposited in an off-shore bank. Unfortunately, I don't think you're quite as amenable to persuasion as your cousin. So this is what we're going to do. You and I will exchange clothes. And poor Billy will shoot you and then himself, after having shot the good doctor down the hall, in a love triangle gone awry." She thought it over and sighed. "This is far too messy for my taste, but I don't see a way out of it. Undress now. Start with your boots."

I bent over toward my right foot. And I pulled the gun out of my boot and shot.

With a small .22 caliber, you have to pray when you shoot. It's the equivalent of throwing a Hail Mary pass in football.

My first shot landed in her right shoulder. Her gun hand wavered.

My second shot grazed her ear.

"Stop." She dropped her gun. Blood ran in one stream

down her arm, in another down her neck and across her collarbone. "Stop."

I kept the gun aimed more or less at her chest. My stomach was churning, and I was tempted to walk out and leave both of them. But I didn't.

"Uncuff Billy and let him call security."

"I'll have to get the key."

"Wrong. Just ungag him, then. You can hit O for Operator, but I want him on the receiver. I don't want you faking the call and somehow alerting a friend instead."

Awkwardly, with her left hand, she loosened Billy's gag, picked up the receiver, hit O, and then held the receiver next to Billy's head.

Hotel security arrived first, then the hotel doctor, followed sometime later by Detective Matthews and the crime team from the Reno Police Department.

I told the story and Billy confirmed it.

Sada was taken into custody.

The first security guard to arrive tossed a clean towel over Billy, but he spent a lot of time naked and cuffed while people walked in and out of the room. If it wasn't Sada's idea of punishment, it was certainly mine. I'd have to think later whether it was enough.

Billy not only gave his own name and address to the police, but Sada's as well. The silent partner no more.

"How long are you planning to stay in Reno?" Matthews asked him. "We'll need your testimony to make the charge stick."

"I'll stay as long as you need me," Billy said. "After all, I have family here."

I winced.

"Yeah, sure," Matthews nodded. He had raised his eyebrows when I introduced Billy as my cousin, but he was now beyond shock. "I won't blame you if you decide not to stay at the hotel after this. But make certain I have a good local address and phone number, okay?"

That was to me as much as to Billy.

I waited until Matthews had left and Billy was dressed before I brought up the question again.

"Where are you going to stay?" I asked.

"I'll have to think about it." He was still badly shaken. "The detective is right. I don't think I want to stay here."

"Do me a favor and sleep on my couch tonight. I don't want to worry that Sada might make a phone call and get somebody to come after you." I was still pissed at Billy for getting me into this, and I wasn't happy with the idea of spending more time with him, but I didn't want to lie awake wondering whether he was going to disappear, whether he wanted to or not.

"Oh, God," he groaned, "she's capable of it."

"Okay. Tonight you sleep on my couch and we'll figure out the rest of it tomorrow. Maybe you could stay with Ramona for a while. Work on your tan."

"Do you have to tell Aunt Ramona what happened?"

"Billy, there was a murder in a hotel-casino. What happened will be in a police report. TV news vans root out crime scenes the way pigs root truffles. I won't be surprised if Ramona knows before I can call her. She watches the eleven o'clock news."

He thought for a moment.

"She'll know about the murder. She might even find out that the railroad tank car situation wasn't quite on the up-and-up. But I was led astray, and I can explain. It's just—she doesn't have to know about Sada, and about me being naked and cuffed, and all that, does she?"

Billy was looking at me with hope in his soft, hazel eyes.

"Maybe, maybe not. I'll have to think about it."

"I'll owe you," he said, starting to twitch. "Remember when I dragged you around the pool? I'll let you drag me around the pool. Any pool in town. What do you say?"

I almost liked the idea. But the thing was, he liked it better. The hope in his soft, hazel eyes was that I would drag him around the pool.

Whatever punishment he wanted, thought he deserved, I wouldn't help him out.

I clapped a hand on his shoulder.

"Hey, Billy, we're family. I forgave you for that a long time ago. And don't worry. Your secret is safe with me."

The hope drained from his eyes, then came back.

"I'll think of something else," he said.

I was uncomfortably aware of the old joke about what the sadist responded when the masochist begged, "Hurt me." But I said it anyway.

"No."

Caught in the Act

A Freddie O'Neal Mystery

Lane Josten was a minor character in The Luck of the Draw, *and I wanted to give him more screen time—or page time, in this case. Since the Freddie O'Neal series was cancelled before I had the chance, the best I could do was offer him a starring role in a short story.*

I could argue that the decline of America as a great power, a symbol of liberty and justice for all, occurred sometime in the years between 1953 and 1980—between *High Noon* and *High Noon II*. In the original, Gary Cooper is the lawman who puts duty before any petty personal considerations. Love has to wait until he shoots Hank Miller dead in order to save the town.

In the so-called sequel, the marshal is greedy and venal, no better—maybe even worse—than the ex-con he is hounding, while Lee Majors, in the former Cooper role, is a righteous man who operates without a badge. The law can no longer be trusted. The good citizen is forced to step in, with nobody discussing the line between the good citizen and the vigilante.

Distrust for law enforcement breeds disorder and decline in the community. And no matter how necessary the original vigilance councils of the West might have been, when we start to prefer them to due process, the barbarians have crashed the gates.

Of course, I could also argue that the causes of disorder in the community are more complex than the plotlines of a couple of old movies, and since I've never made it past the first half hour of *High Noon II*, the ending might undercut my original point.

For the record, I don't believe that my PI license gives me the right to take the law into my own hands. I consider myself an adjunct peace officer, bound by the same laws, if not always by quite the same rules, regulations, and procedures. And I've never personally had a bad experience with the police.

Nevertheless, I know people who have. So I was willing to listen when Lane Josten, anchor of the "Channel 12 News at Eleven," brought me a problem that he really should have taken to someone with a badge instead. Blackmail is, after all, a crime.

Lane and I had a friend in common, journalist Sandra Herrick, who had once been Lane's co-anchor. And I had met him a couple of times when another woman who used to be his co-anchor had been involved with a murder suspect. I had even borrowed his shirt. I hadn't gotten to know him for two reasons. There was a lot else going on in my life at the time, and I'm uncomfortable around men who are not only prettier than I am, they're prettier than any woman all the way up to Cindy Crawford.

His black hair had a glistening wave that didn't quite fall onto his forehead. His face seemed blessed with a permanent ski-bum tan, wide dark eyes that crinkled with smile lines, and a generous mouth that usually gleamed with teeth so aesthetically perfect that the dentist should have signed them. Or maybe had, for all I know. I didn't get that close.

This day, the gleaming teeth were hidden by lips drawn tight in a face so rigid that the tan had cracked into Seurat-sized dots. As he sat across the desk from me, in one of the black-and-white cowhide chairs placed there for clients, he wasn't smiling. The tension and lack of animation added several years to the appearance of perpetual youth he presented on camera. I suspected his birth certificate would confirm that this older Lane Josten was the real one. Even so, he had the most perfect face I had ever seen in the flesh.

"Someone has some pictures of me." His eyes were focused beyond my shoulder at the fish swimming on my computer screen. "The person who has them wants money for them. I want you to make the exchange."

"Why me?"

"I don't want to see him."

That wasn't enough. I waited.

"Because I trust you. You're Sandra's friend." He glanced over at me to see if that meant anything. I nodded and waited some more. "I don't think you'd hurt me."

"What kind of pictures and why are you paying for them?" Whether I was going to hurt him depended on what was going on.

"Pictures of the two of us. Together. And I'm paying for them because he threatened to send copies to Horton Robb if I don't." He glanced at me again, hoping he wouldn't have to get any more explicit, then back to the fish.

Horton Robb was the station owner and general manager. He wasn't known for tolerance. A local joke went that Horton wouldn't have a stereo in his home because it had a left speaker.

"Sandra hasn't talked about you," I said. "In case you were wondering, she didn't betray your confidence."

"I didn't think she would—or at least not without some

good reason." Lane ran his hand through his wave, the only clue that he wasn't just fascinated by the fish.

"Okay. This is extortion. My professional advice is to go to the police, set up a sting, and press charges."

Lane looked down at his hands, away from the cartoon aquarium, and shook his head.

"Okay," I said again. "You don't want to go to the police. What would happen if you simply called the blackmailer's bluff? How bad could it be?"

"The end of my career. Even if Reno could accept a gay news anchor—and I haven't seen any encouraging signs of that—Horton couldn't. He'd demote me to field reporter immediately, even though it's in violation of my contract, and dare me to sue."

"You could sue and win."

"Maybe. And the suit would take years to drag through the courts, and he'd appeal, which would take more years. I wouldn't have a job. And the only person more undesirable than a gay news anchor is a gay news anchor in the middle of a breach of contract lawsuit."

I thought again of Sandra Herrick, who had moved from television to newspapers rather than sue Horton Robb over breaching her contract when she became pregnant. Lane was probably right. Still, I couldn't help wishing somebody would sue Horton.

"You know this, but I'll say it anyway. You'll have no guarantee that you'll receive the only copies of the photos. Even if this person gives me the negatives, he could have contact negatives stashed somewhere. Once you pay a blackmailer, you're setting yourself up for a lifetime of dread. Every time you check the mail, every time you answer the phone, you could get hit again."

"That's why I want you to go. I want you to make it

clear—this is the only time. If he tries again, I'll tell him to go to hell. I'll leave Reno and start over somewhere else before I'll pay another dime."

I had to puzzle over that a minute. "You think he may not believe you—but he'll believe me?"

Lane swiveled around to face me, and his mouth flickered with a ghost of its usual smile. "You're tougher than I am."

I couldn't argue with that. "Set up a meeting. I'll only charge you for the couple of hours it takes to do the job. And I won't threaten him—I'll simply report what you've told me."

He nodded. "That'll do."

It took him a minute to gather the strength to pick up the dark blue jacket draped over his knees and get out of the chair. The late October day was too warm for a jacket, but Lane evidently hadn't watched his own station's weather report the night before. Indian summer, the guy had said.

"How many people know?" I asked.

Lane paused at the door.

"That's hard to say. My friends know—Sandra knows, of course—and I have an occasional drink at Tom Thumb's. Not often."

Tom Thumb's was a bar on South Virginia, a couple of miles past the city limit.

"You thought you could do that and stay in the closet?" I asked.

"I hoped," he answered. He hadn't looked back at me. "I hoped we were all friends."

"I guess this guy isn't the friend you thought he was."

"At least not the friend he used to be."

Lane flashed a half smile over his shoulder and slipped out the door.

I hit a key on my computer to bring back Tetris.

Lane called again two days later to tell me he had set up a meeting. He stopped by my office that afternoon to give me a fat envelope. An address was written on it.

"His name is Jimmy Dahl. He's expecting you at four o'clock."

"How will I know I have all the photos?"

"You won't. I have to trust Jimmy on that." His skin and smile were almost back to normal, but a soft red glow traveled from his neck to his cheekbones. "I'd just as soon you didn't look at them."

"I'll ask him to seal them."

"Thanks." He hesitated, as if there might be something more, then closed it off with a smile.

"I'll call you when I get back," I said.

"Right."

When Lane had gone, I placed the envelope in a zippered leather folder that could hold the photos coming back and checked the address on a map. It was in a rundown area just off Glendale Avenue, between 395 and the Truckee River, ten minutes away at most.

I gave myself twenty.

I parked the Jeep in front of a crumbling stucco six-plex wedged sideways between two clapboard houses of uncertain vintage. Some kind of deciduous tree held out bare limbs as if it didn't know how to react to the sun. I had grabbed a denim jacket as I left the house, out of October habit, but I left it on the seat.

Jimmy Dahl's apartment was number three.

As I started down the walk, a man wearing a tan cowboy hat brushed past. His head was lowered against an imaginary breeze, and I didn't see his face.

When I knocked on the door marked three, and it swung

open at my touch, I had a sinking feeling that I should have been more observant.

The apartment was only a combination living room and sleeping area, with a counter-topped half wall marking where the tiny kitchen area began. The unmade sofa-bed took up most of the room.

And a naked male body on blood-soaked sheets took up most of the bed.

I should have picked up the phone and called the police. I know that. Even if I wanted to protect my client—which I did—I would have had time to look, carefully, for the incriminating photos while I waited for an official response. We could have worked something out.

But adrenaline kicked in, and I raced back to the street to see if I could catch a glimpse of the man in the tan hat.

He was waiting for me, leaning against the leafless tree. Beneath the cowboy hat he was wearing a blue work shirt and boot-cut Wranglers. His face was round, bland, and full of good cheer.

"Pete Lowry," he said, holding out his right hand. A tan cowhide briefcase was in the left. "You're Freddie O'Neal, right?"

"How do you know who I am?"

When he realized I wasn't going to shake, he retrieved his hand and lightly touched his hat brim in what might have been a salute.

"Saw you on television—that nasty bidness at the university."

He actually said "bidness." I don't think even real cowboys say "bidness" when they mean business. And Lowry wasn't a cowboy, he was a private investigator. Even though I hadn't met him, I'd heard the name. He'd retired under unspecified pressure after not quite twenty years on the Las

Vegas police force and moved to Reno. A Las Vegas PI had e-mailed me to be careful if I ran into him.

"What are you doing here?"

Lowry pointed to the leather folder under my arm. "I suspect we're here for similar reasons. The unfortunate young man in number three had some photographs that a client of mine was willing to pay good money for."

"So what have you got in your briefcase?" I realized when I said it that I was pushing, but I didn't think he'd pull out a gun and shoot me on the sidewalk. Not that the man on the bed had been shot. Even though I hadn't looked closely, I was sure there was too much blood for that. And none of it was on Lowry.

"Well, little lady, I'm afraid I can't let you see that." I must have frowned, because he added, "Figure of speech, no offense. I took the time to find the pictures I came for, and I don't think my client would approve if I showed them to you."

"If you have the pictures—and you didn't kill Dahl—why did you wait for me?"

"If you'd called the police, what's the first thing you would have said?"

"I saw a man leaving the scene."

He nodded, smiling again. "There you go. Thought I'd save you the trouble of looking through mug shots."

"And save yourself the trouble of defending why you left a crime scene without reporting it. Which is what we have to do right now."

"After you."

I turned back toward the building, but stopped short as a beefy man wearing tight slacks and a loose jacket walked up. This one I knew. His face was red, and he had to be sweating into his shoulder holster.

"Hello, Crane," I said. "You know Lowry?"

"O'Neal." He nodded at me, then glanced at Lowry and added, "I haven't had the pleasure."

Crane didn't look like it was a pleasure. Neither did Lowry, who gripped his briefcase a little tighter even as he smiled.

"Pete Lowry, Barry Crane," I said. "Lowry and I both have clients facing an extortion threat from one Jimmy Dahl. You too?"

"So it seems," Crane said, "so it seems."

For a moment I couldn't figure why they were both doing the puffed chest routine instead of shaking hands like colleagues. Even if Crane had heard of Lowry and didn't like the information, it would have been like him to offer a damp palm. Then I remembered that my client and the dead man were both gay. I'd make book that their clients were as well. Neither of these guys would refuse anybody's money, but they each evidently felt some tension over this one.

"There's a dead body in number three," I said.

"What?" Crane jerked around, the loser in the staredown.

"I'm going back to call the police."

Maybe they didn't want to touch each other, but they were both willing to touch me. A moist, heavy hand fell on my right shoulder, a dry one on my left.

"Let's not be too hasty," Lowry said. "After all, we have our clients to consider."

"And if that dead body is Jimmy Dahl, our clients are suspects," Crane added. "All three of our clients. Which means giving information about them to the police."

"Information they paid us—and were willing to concede to extortion demands from Jimmy Dahl—to keep secret," Lowry finished.

"Yeah, but then it wasn't murder," I said, brushing both hands away.

"Think for a moment, lit—O'Neal," Lowry said, tipping his hand to his hat again. "Our clients will be ruined. And at least two of them unnecessarily. Maybe all three are innocent. Who knows how many poor wretches were victimized by that Jimmy Dahl?"

"I want to see the corpse," Crane said. "After that, we talk. I don't think we want to rush our clients into the hands of the police."

I wasn't happy about this. Nevertheless, I led the way back to number three.

Jimmy Dahl's body was still on the bed, slowly cooling to ivory. A jagged wound on his chest looked as if someone had stuck a knife right below the breastbone and twisted. From the condition of the sheets and walls, the blood had spurted and pumped before he died. His face had the glazed, gaping expression of a small rabbit caught on the highway. He had seen the weapon and known it was the end.

There wasn't room for all three of us in the doorway. I walked around to the other side of the bed, where all I could see was an ear and the back of his head. He'd had dark hair, already thinning.

"My guy didn't do this," Crane said. "Hasn't the guts."

"I'd say my client is off the hook for the same reason," Lowry said, apparently happy to go along.

They had each taken a position at maximum distance from each other and the bed. In the tiny space available, they could still have held hands.

"Bullshit. Everybody's a suspect until we start establishing alibis."

"Then you agree?" Lowry asked. "No police?"

"I don't agree. But I'll go this far—we take the photos we came for, and we ask whoever shows from the police if we can report to our clients tonight and go in for a formal statement in the morning. I think we can get away with that much, and it gives us each a little time to check out our own clients. Maybe we can protect a couple of innocent people that way."

"Way to go," Lowry said.

"Where'd you find the photos?" I asked.

"What?" Crane turned sharply, and for a minute I thought he was going to grab Lowry's neck. He pulled a handkerchief from his jacket and wiped his forehead.

"In the dresser," Lowry said. "Second drawer."

A dresser with a Scotch tape dispenser, a stapler, some pens, and a few scattered window envelopes on top—the kind that hold bills—was at the foot of the bed. The angled mirror reflected Dahl from the torn chest down. I had to turn away.

Lowry had either been lucky with his first try or he had tossed the place carefully. Not that there were many places to look. For all the personal effects showing, Dahl could have been packed and out of there in ten minutes. Aside from the shirt, jeans, and jockey shorts lying on a chair, and a coffee mug on the small table, everything but the bed itself was as void of character as a motel room. A second coffee mug was in the drainer next to the sink.

"Did you leave prints?" I asked.

"Not a chance." As I started for the dresser, Lowry added, "I didn't leave any photos, either."

Crane hitched his shoulders. "Let's have 'em."

"Easy, now," Lowry said. He placed the briefcase on the carpet, held out his hands in a gesture of surrender, then knelt down and flipped the catch to reveal a stack of tan envelopes. "Four—count 'em—four. One marked Lowry, one marked O'Neal, one marked Crane, and one marked Dennis."

"Why do you have them? Who the hell is Dennis?" Crane asked.

"Why the hell didn't you tell me you had mine?"

"I have them because I wanted to get them out of the apartment. I wouldn't have let you get away without your envelopes. I was just playing it out." Lowry's geniality seemed to be wearing thin as he handed a fat nine-by-twelve to me and another to Crane. "As for Dennis—if he doesn't show up, I say let's open his."

"I'm Dennis. Open what?"

A slender young man with streaked blond hair curling around his chin stood in the doorway. When Crane turned to look at him, he cleared a line of sight to the body on the bed.

"Oh, my God." The young man blanched so quickly that I thought we might have a second corpse on our hands. He caught himself against the wall. "What happened?"

"Somebody decided murder was cheaper than blackmail," I said. "Did you know the deceased or were you hired?"

"Know Jimmy? Of course I knew Jimmy. Who are you? Where are the police?" He glanced from face to face, shock turning to terror.

"I'm calling them right now," I said.

Before anyone could protest, I picked up the phone on the dresser—using fingertips and hoping I wouldn't smudge anything—and punched out the direct dial to Detectives.

I was lucky enough to catch Matthews. He didn't think it was so lucky. But he said he'd be right over.

"What happened?" Dennis asked again. While I was on

the phone, he had moved over to the bed. He had taken the envelope Lowry held out, automatically, without looking. It dangled at his side.

"We've each been hired to make an exchange—money for photographs. This is what we found," I said. "And you?"

"I thought I could talk him out of doing this. Oh, Jimmy." Dennis began to slump, and I grabbed his arm to keep him from the bloody sheets.

Crane and Lowry both backed toward the door. They stopped when they reached it at the same time.

"Waiting outside is a good idea," I said. "We'll all wait outside."

Crane let Lowry go first.

"I'd rather wait here," Dennis said.

His eyes were filling, and I wished I could let him mourn in peace.

"Sorry. We're messing up a crime scene."

"A crime scene. But that man had the envelopes. Doesn't a crime scene mean we have to give the envelopes to the police?"

"It means we're working in a gray area here." My nose should have grown longer on that one. I turned him toward the door. "If the photos are evidence—if they provide a motive for murder—we'll have to turn them over. Do you have a way to carry your envelope?"

"I don't understand."

"Well, if you wave it in Detective Matthews' face, he'll have to ask you what's in it." I pulled the corner of the envelope containing what I hoped were photos and negatives of Lane Josten out of the leather folder.

Dennis seemed puzzled for a moment. Then he handed his envelope to me.

"How do I get it back?"

"We'll leave separately, and I'll meet you."

"Tom Thumb's," he said, "I need a drink."

Not the place I would have chosen, but I didn't want to argue.

I hadn't realized how cool the apartment was until we were back on the sidewalk. The sun was heavy on my cotton shirt, and I envied Lowry his hat.

The four of us waited quietly for Matthews. No envelopes in sight.

A black-and-white arrived first. Two unmarked cars rolled up right behind.

If Matthews had been unhappy when I called, that was nothing to his reaction when he was faced with three private investigators who didn't want to divulge their clients' names plus one private citizen who admitted to being a friend of the deceased but was otherwise unwilling to volunteer anything. He finally agreed to let Crane, Lowry, and me come in for formal statements the next morning, making dire threats about what would happen to our licenses if we failed to show. He was still talking to Dennis, who gave his last name as Stiers and his occupation as accountant, when we left.

I swung by my office to drop off Lane's envelope. I didn't want to carry it with me to the bar. I thought about calling him, but it was after five-thirty, and telling him Dahl had been murdered ten minutes before he went on camera didn't seem the thing to do. If I caught him at seven, he'd have four hours to compose himself before the late news. The risk was that the police beat reporter would tell him first. I decided to chance it.

I got back in the Jeep, took a couple of quick corners, and headed south on Virginia Street.

Tom Thumb's was a squat, brown rectangle in the middle of a parking lot. The neon sign above the door was small and pale. This wasn't a place anyone would drop into, not without knowing what it was.

I had thought Dennis Stiers might beat me there, but none of the startled male faces that caught my entrance belonged to that particular young man. I had my own moment of surprise, though. Barry Crane was seated at the bar. He wiped his forehead when he saw me heading toward him.

"This isn't what you're thinking, O'Neal," he said, as I settled onto the next stool.

"Okay. I'm not thinking. But I'm listening."

"Buy you a drink?"

"Beer's fine. Whatever's on tap."

The bartender had been busy with a blender concoction for a couple at the far end of the counter. Crane caught his eye, held up his own glass, and two fingers.

Crane didn't say anything until the glasses were in front of us.

"Freddie O'Neal, I want you to meet Barry Crane, Jr. My son."

"Pleased to meet you," the bartender said. "Although I'm sorry about the circumstances."

"Same here."

"I haven't told the other customers about Jimmy. I'd rather they found out from someone else. I wasn't fond of him, but other people thought he was attractive. That's how all this happened."

I hadn't noticed the resemblance until the bartender started talking. Barry Junior was younger and thinner and had more hair, but the timbre in his voice was similar. When his father frowned at him, he excused himself to wash glasses out of earshot.

"I'm still listening," I said.

"Dahl was threatening to out a local attorney. Barry asked me to intercede. I don't even know the attorney's name—that's why I'm here."

"It may be time to open the envelope," I said.

Crane thought for a moment, then pulled the envelope out of his jacket. He must have had a pocket in the lining. I caught a glimpse of his shoulder holster as he shifted. I had been right—he was carrying.

"I'll let him do it." Crane gave the envelope a shove down the counter. It stopped near his son.

Barry Junior dried his hands and picked it up. He moved back to us.

"My friend wouldn't have killed Jimmy," he said. "He was just going to pay. He didn't even want to hire help."

"We want you to make sure those are your friend's pictures," I prompted.

The envelope had been sealed with Scotch tape. Barry Junior picked up a knife and slit the top. He fumbled with the contents.

"The pictures are here. The negatives aren't."

"Warned you," Crane said.

"Hell." I wanted to say something more profound. But I had warned Lane, too.

"I guess you didn't get there in time."

I thought Barry Junior was saying that to me, and I was about to bristle and tell him I was early, when I realized that Dennis was standing next to me. I hadn't heard him come in.

"No, I didn't."

"What time were you supposed to be there?" I asked.

"No special time," Dennis answered. "Jimmy said he was setting up appointments at four, four-thirty, and five. I didn't know they were with private investigators. I thought he was dealing directly with friends."

"Former friends," I said.

Dennis nodded. He took a sip of the beer that Barry Junior placed in front of him.

"There was an envelope for you but you didn't have an appointment?"

"No. I had told him I wouldn't pay. I was ready to leave the closet anyway. There was nothing he could do to me. Jimmy said in that case, he'd let me have the pictures. He planned to leave town once he got the money, so he didn't have any use for them."

"He had use for something," Crane grumbled. "Why else would he keep the negatives?"

"Keep the negatives? He wasn't going to keep the negatives."

I handed Dennis his envelope. He ripped it apart and spread the photographs on the bar. I caught a glimpse of two naked male bodies in awkward positions and looked away. Crane almost fell off the stool turning his back.

"You're right," Dennis said. "The negatives are missing."

"What time was your appointment?" I asked Crane.

"Four-thirty. I came early to check things out. Lowry must have done the same."

"Shit. The last shall be first," I said. "Clean and dry, too."

"What?"

"Have you got a phone directory?" I asked Barry Junior.

"The public phone is by the john," he said, pointing to the back of the barroom.

One glance told me the directory was too old to give me what I wanted. I left without saying good-bye.

I made it back to my office in record time.

Lowry's ad in the Yellow Pages listed a post office box. The reverse directory gave me an address in Sparks.

I wanted to leave again immediately, but I restrained myself long enough to call Matthews.

"Did someone take a shower?" I asked.

"What? A shower? Yeah. The bathroom was wet. We've even got what is maybe the perp's hair from a towel. Why?"

"I'll call you later." I would have asked him to meet me, but I wanted to be sure I was right first.

I made it to the Sparks address in record time, too.

Lowry was tossing a duffel bag into the trunk of an old Pontiac when I blocked the driveway with my Jeep.

"That's not a good place to park, little lady." He smiled, sort of. I didn't exactly feel welcome.

"I'll move it when the police arrive," I said, wishing I'd given Matthews more information.

"And when's that going to be? Seems to me you'd have to offer something to get them over here, and I just don't think you're holding any cards."

"Maybe. But I know you're holding the negatives—and that's extortion."

"Who'd I threaten? And that's only assuming you're right. You could get me for taking them from the crime scene, but we'll all get our wrists slapped for that one. So get out of my way, O'Neal." He shifted restlessly.

"Let me tell you what I think." What I really thought was that I should have brought Crane with me. "I think nobody hired you—Dahl had pictures of you. That was why you resigned from the force and left Las Vegas—somebody was threatening to out you. You made a five o'clock appointment to meet Dahl, but you got there early, had a cup of coffee, offered to make up, do it once more for old times' sake. He gave you your envelope, so you knew where they were. You didn't have to toss the place. Thus, no worry about fingerprints. Once you had the pictures, you both got naked, and you killed him."

Lowry wasn't even trying to smile anymore.

I took a deep breath and continued. "You took a shower and cleaned up, then removed the negatives from the other envelopes and resealed them with tape. Maybe you were going to leave them, creating as many suspects as possible. For some reason you changed your mind and put them in your briefcase. Maybe you didn't want to risk a possible fingerprint on the tape. You were on your way out, planning to return at five in all innocence, when you ran into me."

The sun was fading into twilight, but even in shadow I could see his face mottling with dark streaks of anger.

"Wrong from the start, little lady." His voice was low and controlled. "I didn't know the fag. And I sure as hell didn't get into trouble over my sexual orientation. I was hired by a local politico who knew I'd been pushed off the force in Las Vegas for getting a little too excited during a couple of arrests. He'd heard I needed money, and he thought paying once for a hit would be cheaper than paying forever for the negatives."

"Not a good choice."

"Well, it might have been, but I decided a better choice for me was taking the hit money and then going for the retirement pay. I figured with four professionals involved—I thought I had Dennis Whosit, too—I'd get money more regular than Social Security." He was relaxing a little, and the smile was back.

"So how'd you get naked?"

Lowry offered a low chuckle.

"Hell, I pretended he was a girl till his pants were off.

Told him how cute he was, all that. I could have just shot him—would have been neater—but I liked the idea of making it look like a crime of passion." He shifted his weight restlessly again. "It's been fun talking with you, O'Neal. You are a smart woman, and I surely wish I hadn't cut the time so close. It's going to be a lot harder collecting my Social Security on the run. Now you got a choice. You move the Jeep and let me leave, or I break your neck."

I know a little about self-defense, and I might have been able to take him if he rushed me. I didn't want to try. As he moved forward, I made a dive for the lawn, rolled over, and came up with my gun in my hand.

"Where the hell did that pea shooter come from?"

"My boot. It's small and not too accurate, but you'll have to get your hands on me to break my neck. That's close enough that I could put a hole in yours. You can take the chance, or you can climb into the trunk of your car and pull it shut. I figure the police will get here before you suffocate."

He struggled with the idea, but he finally turned toward the car, chuckling. He put one boot, then the other, into the trunk.

"You're going to have a hell of a time proving anything," he said. "I'll deny everything but taking the envelopes. Hearsay evidence never hanged anybody. The rest is circumstantial. Nothing ties me to the murder. No weapon, no prints, no nothing."

He had to take his hat off to get all the way inside. I waited until he had closed the lid. Then I sat on it to make sure the latch had caught before I yelled to him.

"You forgot something at the scene, Lowry! Use your head!"

He had left the front door open, so I made two calls

from his phone, one to the television station and one to the police. I caught Lane just as he was coming off the set, told him not to worry, and arranged to meet him after he was through for the night.

Matthews was still unhappy with me, but he cheered up when I went with him to the station.

I told him most of the truth.

Lane was waiting for me in a quiet corner of the Comstock Room on the top floor of the Mother Lode casino by the time I arrived, a little after midnight. He looked tired, but relieved. He even managed a gleaming smile when I slid into the booth next to him and passed him the envelope.

"I didn't look at the pictures. And I didn't sort out the negatives. I trust you'll do that and return the ones not yours to the people who need them."

"Won't you get into trouble over this?" he asked.

"I hope not. Lowry's briefcase was sitting on the front seat of the car, unlocked, and he hadn't bothered to seal the envelope he was keeping. So the police will find an envelope with pictures of Jimmy Dahl in a compromising position with the man who hired the hit. If Lowry volunteers that he took the negatives, he may have to volunteer a whole lot more. And trying to make a plea bargain by offering to testify that I rifled his briefcase wouldn't get him very far. I suspect that Matthews isn't going to try too hard to make life difficult for anyone but Lowry."

Lane picked up my hand and kissed it. Then he closed his eyes and held my hand against his cheek.

"I can't begin to tell you how grateful I am," he said softly.

"Lane, hello. Grabbing a late night snack?" A deep voice rumbled over my shoulder. "And Miss O'Neal, isn't it?"

"Horton. Sure." Lane turned a soft shade of red and dropped my hand.

"Hi," I said.

"No problem," Horton chuckled. "What you do on your own time is your own business."

"Thanks," Lane said. Once Horton had moved away, he added, "Is this going to be a problem for you?"

"Not at all." I noticed a flash a few tables away, and I motioned for the club photographer to come over to the booth. "Make it good," I told her.

I didn't have to tell Lane what I wanted.

I checked with Matthews the next morning. Lowry was keeping his mouth shut, as I had figured. No mention of negatives or rifled briefcases. They had taken some hair samples for laboratory testing. The politician in the photos was coming in with his lawyer that afternoon. Matthews was almost cheerful.

The photo from the Mother Lode arrived in the mail a few days later. I framed it and hung it on my office wall.

So now anybody who walks in can see the handsomest man in Reno caught in the act of kissing me.

That's my idea of justice.

Self-Defense

This was originally a chapter in a novel, but the first two friends who read it both said that it was too long a break in the action, and that the protagonist's self-defense class would have to take place off-stage, as it were. I reluctantly agreed, and then turned it into a short story, which turned out to be my first fiction sale. Another friend submitted it to Network, *a feminist fiction magazine that is no longer around, and they published it in 1990. With the advantage of twelve years' experience, I've rewritten it for this collection.*

"A woman in the United States is raped every two minutes," the instructor shouted. "In the three hours we will be together this morning, ninety women will be raped. And another ninety will be raped this afternoon. Rape does not just happen at night—we all think we are safer during the day—rape happens all the time! Look at the woman to your right, look at the woman to your left. Statistically, half of the women in this room—living in Los Angeles—will be raped sometime during their lives. According to FBI figures, one out of three women in the United States will be raped."

Jessie and Karen glanced uncomfortably at each other and then at the women on their other sides, who also glanced and turned quickly away. The woman on Jessie's right looked tough—those were well-defined biceps under a "Take Back the Night" t-shirt. She didn't look as if she needed a self-defense workshop. But even so she glanced away.

Jessie wondered what had happened to bring this woman here. Something had happened, surely. Something had surely happened to each of them, except Karen, who had agreed to go because Jessie didn't want to go alone.

The instructor shouted on. "Each of you—because of the kind of woman you are—has discouraged at least one rape. You have discouraged a rapist because of the way you walk, because of the way you answered when he asked you a question, because you were not *compliant!*"

There were some murmurs from the group. These women were not compliant. After all, they were here.

"What are the common myths about rape?" the instructor shouted.

"Women ask for it!" the woman to Jessie's right growled.

"Right!"

"Rape is an act of passion," Jessie volunteered.

"Right!"

"Most rapists are strangers," another woman called out.

"Rape is a good way of punishing uppity women," spat still another.

The pitch of the answers rose higher, the rate of response faster.

"Women secretly *want* to be raped," came a cry from the back.

"Right!" shouted the instructor. "Right! Right!"

Jessie's heart began to beat in rhythm to the shouts.

"Another myth is that you will be hurt worse if you fight back." The instructor paced the room, looking each woman in the eye. "Most rapists look for the easiest possible target. They *want* compliant women! Women who don't know how to say *NO!* The rapist of a young Asian woman was found not guilty by a jury, just because she never said the word *NO!* He claimed he didn't know she was resisting! Well, she didn't know *how* to say *NO!* And some of you may not have learned to say *NO!* But you're not going to be victims! And even if you have been before, you're not going to be again!"

She looked at Jessie on that one. Jessie had to look away.

"No matter what happened to you, no matter what brought you to this class, it wasn't your fault." The instructor moved on to the next woman. "Whatever it was, if you were attacked, if you were mugged, if you were raped, you were not to blame. You didn't know how to protect yourself. And now you're going to learn. You're going to learn to say *NO!* A victim doesn't say *NO!* But you are not a victim, and if you were one, you aren't one anymore. You will say *NO!* Now, let me hear it!"

"No," a few of the women said uneasily.

"Louder!" shouted the instructor.

The "nos" became a little stronger.

"Let me hear it *louder! NO! NO!*" The instructor led them, turning it into a chant.

"NO! NO! NO! NO!"

"And that's just the way you're going to shout it when you attack Ralph the Rapist!" The instructor held up a pair of stuffed jeans. "You will note that Ralph has no chest. In the movies, you see women struggling with men and hitting them in the chest. Those movies were made by *men!* Men don't want you to know how to hurt them. Never hit a man in the chest. You won't hurt him. And if you're going to hit him, you've got to want to hurt him. The chest, the upper body, is his strongest area. But your center of gravity is lower. You're going to learn today to use your strength against his weakness. You're going to learn all the vulnerable areas—the eyes, the ears, the nose, the balls, and the kneecaps."

"The kneecaps?" Jessie asked.

"Absolutely! The average man's kneecap breaks under forty pounds of pressure. The average *untrained* woman can smash down with a force of sixty pounds. That's one and a half kneecaps. And you're going to learn how to do it today! But we're going to start top down—with the eyes. Pick a partner."

Jessie turned to Karen, who shrugged and nodded. The other women—about a dozen—paired off. Following instructions, one woman from each pair picked up a pillow from a stack in the middle of the room and held it for the other to hit.

Karen held the pillow at arm's length, eye level, with her head turned away, as if she were afraid Jessie might miss. Jessie knew she wouldn't miss. But she had to try it first, see how it felt to hit the pillow, so she punched it with a soft jab, an embarrassingly soft jab. Then she tried really hitting it. Almost. She began hitting the pillow harder and harder, annoyed that Karen was holding it so limply, as if it weren't a symbol of oppression at all. She finally knocked it out of Karen's hands.

"Great! Keep it up!"

The instructor had noticed. Jessie, pleased, hit the pillow out of Karen's hands again. She found it more awkward when she tried to scratch the pillow's eyes or break its eardrums. But hitting it on the nose felt good.

Karen couldn't knock the pillow out of Jessie's hands. Jessie shook it at her, to encourage her, but Karen never put any weight into her blows.

"This is weird," Karen whispered when the instructor called a break. "I need a cigarette. You coming?"

Jessie shook her head. She wanted to ask Karen why she had come if she wasn't really going to do it. But she knew why Karen had come. Jessie had asked, and Karen was compliant.

Jessie stayed in the bare room, stretching her muscles and looking at the clock, fretting when the break ran past its allotted ten minutes.

Then they were back, and the instructor lined them up. One at a time, they ran at Ralph the Rapist, kicking at his kneecaps, shouting *"NO!"* with each kick.

Then his balls, they started kicking his balls. The balls were harder to hit.

"Men will tell you not to try for the balls, that they protect their balls, that you can't hurt them there. This is a lie! But you have to practice!" the instructor shouted.

They lined up again. The room was large enough to accommodate a much larger class, but Jessie was glad there were so few of them. More practice. This time, her kick landed. Ralph the Rapist went flying. Off balance, Jessie did, too.

"Great! Next time you'll stay on your feet!"

She did, but she missed his balls. Annoyed, she pivoted and smashed his kneecap. The instructor cackled.

"Now, this time, you're going to go for the balls with your hands. Like this." The instructor held Ralph in one hand, demonstrating slowly with the other. "Slap! Grab! Squeeze! Pull! Got that? Watch it again. Slap! Grab! Squeeze! Pull! Say it with me. Slap! Grab! Squeeze! Pull! Now again, faster, louder. *SLAP! GRAB! SQUEEZE! PULL!*"

Jessie felt perspiration soaking the armpits and back of

her t-shirt and starting to dampen the crotch of her jeans. She wished that Ralph really had balls to grab, so she would know for sure she had hit them. The instructor told them that Ralph had originally been anatomically correct, but his balls had long since been lost in the stuffing. Jessie was annoyed that no one had bothered to replace them.

Shortly after noon, they broke for lunch. There was a courtyard behind the small building, nothing more than three picnic tables and a tree. Jessie had promised Karen that she would take care of lunch—chicken salad, bread, cheese, pears, mineral water. The woman with biceps, Sarah, and her pillow-punching partner Rita, a young black woman with hair in cornrows and a lean, gymnast's body, sat at the same table. They had each brought a sandwich and bought a soda from a battered machine near the door.

Jessie had barely taken a bite of her lunch when Sarah plunged into the story of the attack that had brought her to the class.

"I kept screaming and flailing at him as he banged my head against the sidewalk," Sarah was saying as the instructor joined them, pulling an apple and mineral water out of a paper bag. "And—I'm really sorry to say this, Rita—but for weeks afterward I couldn't look at a black man, any black man, without wanting to cry, or scream, or run, or something, I didn't know what."

Rita shrugged. "I know a few black men I'd run away from. You were lucky he didn't have a knife."

"I know a few white men I'd run from," Karen said, smiling at them.

Jessie looked at the bit of mayonnaise-smeared chicken on her plastic fork. She didn't understand how Karen could wolf chicken salad and nod sympathetically at the same time.

"Yeah, I know." Sarah's voice was flat. "But if it happens again, I'll be ready for him, knife or no knife."

"I'm sure it won't happen again," Karen said. "Why should it?"

Sarah smiled a little lopsidedly at her. "Why should it happen the first time?"

"Nobody can promise it won't happen again, you know that," the instructor said. She was short and heavy, as if she normally ate more than an apple for lunch. She had strong features and might have been attractive if she had wanted to be. But nobody looked attractive in a self-defense class.

"All I can promise is that you will be more cautious and you'll be better equipped, if somebody tries it again," she continued. "Although you might want to think twice about fighting if he has a knife. You'd have to use your own judgment."

"Yeah, that's what I tell my boyfriend, I gotta use my own judgment," Rita said. "He didn't want me to take this class, but I told him I gotta learn to protect myself. He didn't think I could learn much in one day. Well, he sure has a surprise coming!"

The instructor shook her head. "Don't do it. Women leave this class, and they go home, and there's a man waiting for them. And he says, 'What did you learn?' And she says, 'I learned to protect myself.' He says, 'Sure you did. Prove it. Protect yourself against me.' And he goes for her. And she doesn't want to hurt him. So she can't hit him, she can't break his hold, she can't throw him. She can't hurt someone she loves, so she thinks she can't hurt someone who threatens her. And her power is lost all over again. So don't do it. Practice with each other, take another class, but just tell the man you love that you had a good time today."

"Suppose I wanted to take another class. Where would I go?" Jessie asked.

"There's a place on the Westside, run by women. I'll give you their card when we go back in. Most martial arts places are run by men, and they're pretty condescending toward women who come in."

"Thanks," Jessie said. "I'd like the card."

"Really?" Karen was surprised.

"Yeah, really."

"But after that whole thing with Greg, after you broke up and he—because he—" Karen stopped as Jessie stared at her.

"So?"

"I just have trouble seeing you into violence."

"I'm not into violence. I'm into protecting myself from violence." Even as she said it, Jessie remembered the rush she felt when her foot had connected with the dummy's kneecap. She wanted that rush again.

Karen looked away. Sarah nodded.

After lunch there were chokeholds and bear hugs to break. They learned how to throw a man who pinned them down. Jessie was pleased when Karen threw her. Karen laughed and wanted to do it again.

The class ended at four. The women hugged each other and wished each other well before they dispersed.

Jessie's muscles had started to stiffen by the time they reached Karen's house. She had pulled over on the way, to put the top up on her convertible. The slight breeze made her shiver as her sweat dried, even though the sun was still warm.

When they reached the house, Karen invited Jessie in for a drink.

"Jesus, you both stink," Wayne, Karen's husband, said

in welcome. "Sit down, and I'll get you some wine."

Jessie and Karen slumped in their chairs.

"So what did you learn?" Wayne asked, handing them their glasses.

"Oh, God, it was great. Thanks," Karen said, taking a sip of her wine. "We learned so much. Where to hit, how to hit, how to get away, how to throw somebody who pins you down."

"What?"

"We had a good time," Jessie said.

"No, come on. How to throw somebody who pins you down? Come on, Karen. If I pinned you down, you couldn't throw me. You just aren't strong enough."

"Yes. Yes, I could. I could throw you. I could use my strength against your weakness and throw you."

"Try it," Wayne said, setting down his glass.

"Wayne, forget it, we had a good time," Jessie told him.

"No. Put your glass down, Karen."

"Sure. Okay."

Karen lay down on the floor, and Wayne sat on her, pinning her wrists. They were still for a moment, and then Karen started straining. She struggled with her hand, kicked out with her feet.

"I don't remember," she finally said. "I don't remember how to do it."

"Yeah. I didn't think so." Wayne got to his feet and winked at Jessie.

"Pin me down," Jessie said softly.

Wayne shrugged. "Okay. If you want."

Wayne sat on her easily, holding her wrists tightly, but still smiling.

Jessie lifted her knees, thrust with her pelvis, and stuck her left wrist out. Wayne was suddenly on his back.

He lay there stunned for an instant.

"Let's try that again," he said as he got up.

This time Jessie could feel the tension in his thigh muscles as he braced himself, and he pulled her shoulders as he stretched her arms out. Her wrists hurt from his grip. His eyes narrowed and his lips tightened as he looked down at her. She thrust with her pelvis. And she threw him.

"I guess you did learn something, Jessie, didn't you?" His mouth smiled again.

"I guess I did."

"Excuse me a moment."

Wayne walked down the hall toward the bathroom.

Jessie looked at her untouched wine. "Well. I guess I'd better go now. Thanks for the drink."

Karen walked her to the door.

"Are you sure you don't want to stay?"

"I really need to get home." Jessie said it politely. She didn't want to hurt Karen.

"Oh. Sure. I'm tired, too. I'm—maybe we ought to practice on each other sometime."

"Yeah. That's a good idea. Let's do that."

"Jessie?"

"Yeah?"

"I'm sorry."

"I'm sorry, too."

Jessie had a muddled sense that they were sorry for the wrong things.

Karen reached out and hugged her tightly. Jessie hugged back the best that she could.

"Do you want to call me about the martial arts classes?" Karen asked. "Maybe I could go with you."

"Sure. Of course I'll call you."

Jessie separated herself carefully. She turned back and

waved good-bye as she reached her car.

She had intended to go straight home, but the more she thought about the way Karen had lost her power, had become compliant, and the more she thought about how good it had felt to throw Wayne, the more she felt there was a stop she needed to make first.

And really, Greg's apartment wasn't that far out of the way.

She could feel her heart beating, her blood pounding, as she parked the car in front of his building, as she walked up the stairs to his apartment.

"Jessie!" he exclaimed, startled, when he opened the door to see her there. He was in his bathrobe, towel around his neck, hair still damp from the shower. "Listen, this isn't a good time to talk."

"I didn't exactly come to talk," she said softly. "I came to say *NO!*"

He wasn't expecting it, of course, and that was in her favor. And he was naked under his robe.

Still, Jessie was surprised at how easily she found them with her left hand. Slap! Grab! Squeeze! Pull!

Her right hand became a fist that connected squarely with his nose.

Greg crumpled so easily, barely making a sound, just a whimper as she let go and he belatedly moved to protect himself, curling into a fetal position in the doorway. His face was stark white, bloodless from the shock.

One of his legs had come out from under the bathrobe as he twitched on the floor, and Jessie considered stomping the exposed kneecap. She shook her head. Not this time.

She walked back down the stairs to her car, right hand aching from the force of the blow to his face.

Greg wouldn't leave it there, she knew that. He'd come

after her, worse than the last time. But when he came for her, she would be ready. A knife? No, a gun would be better. More certain.

It was a matter of self-defense.

Defrauding the Cat

A Faith Cassidy Mystery

This story was Faith Cassidy's first appearance in print. I had written several stories about Los Angeles, with the thought that sometime I would turn them into a book, following the lives of three interconnected women. None of the stories were published in their original forms. But when I received an invitation to contribute a story to an anthology about cats and Hollywood, I had to have a protagonist who wasn't Freddie O'Neal. Freddie and Hollywood just couldn't get together. So I called on Faith Cassidy, the actress turned therapist. Here is her first adventure as an amateur sleuth.

"Tell me again. What were you doing with twenty-five thousand dollars in your checking account?" Faith started to lean on the round white table, which rocked just enough to slosh cappuccino into her saucer. She stuck her napkin under the cup and crossed her arms instead.

Sitting in the open area at the Farmers Market always sounded better than it seemed once she got there, particularly in June, when the low cloud cover that marked the beginning of summer in Los Angeles cast a pale gray light on what would otherwise be stalls of brightly colored fruits and vegetables. The tables next to the food stands were surprisingly full, considering the lack of sun. Fluorescent t-shirts saying I SURVIVED THE 6.8 marked the tourists. The native Southern Californians all wore multiple earrings and looked hung over.

"Elizabeth's contract. For the commercial. The money was only supposed to be in the checking account temporarily."

"Right."

"And it wasn't taken. The bank was worried about the amount of the check, so when the commodities firm called them to make certain it was good, they called to make sure I had written it, which of course I hadn't. So they didn't pay it. The money is still there." Michael had been holding his cup until he was certain the table was through rocking. He placed it carefully in the pristine saucer.

"Does it ever bother you to live off Elizabeth like this? You've let your practice go to hell."

"My practice hasn't gone to hell. My clients were all cured. The two I still have only see me once a week out of habit, because they like to talk to me. I'd end the dependency, but they're both so entertaining that I'd miss them. And of course it doesn't bother me to live off Elizabeth. After all, I paid six hundred dollars for her. She wasn't even two months old, and I knew she was going to be a star."

"Michael, she was a kitten. How could you know she was going to grow up with an attitude?"

"Because she was my kitten, Fay. She was therefore going to damn well have my attitude."

"Faith. How many times do I have to tell you—I don't want to be called Fay anymore." She started to lean on the table again, but remembered in time. "I want to be called Faith. It's not such a great leap, from Fay to Faith. It's not as if I wanted to be called Hope or Charity or anything like that."

"Hope would have made more sense. Hope is what you need, not Faith," Michael said cheerfully, impervious to the glare he got in response. "I've been calling you Fay for too many years now. I'm sorry. And I don't understand why you have this sudden need to change your name."

"Because I'm claiming my own identity. People should be named what they want to be named, not stuck with whatever name their parents happened to stick them with. If you wanted to change your name, I would change what I called you."

"Michaelmas, perhaps? Michelangelo? I rather like that."

"Michelangelo it is, then. Anyway, start again from the beginning. I don't understand how this happened."

"Really, I don't either." Michael sighed. "But someone who knew how much money I had in my checking account called the bank and told them I had moved, that I needed new checks sent to my new address, and the bank actually sent them. Sent new checks, ordered in the proper number sequence, to the new address. The recipient then wrote a check to Max Strother Commodities in the amount of twenty-five thousand dollars, to open a trading account. Then the bank called to make certain that I was opening an account at Max Strother Commodities—and astoundingly, inefficiently, called my real telephone number, not the new one the thief had given them, which was the only thing that tripped up whoever wanted to pull this thing off."

"How much did the thief know about you?"

"My Social Security number, my mother's maiden name, and the date and amount of my last deposit." Michael paused to watch the pigeons descend on a half-eaten croissant that a young man two tables away had tossed to the concrete. "I really, truly want it to be an inside job, someone with access to the bank computer. Because if it isn't, the only other people who had that information are my mother, Elizabeth's agent, and Jason."

"Jason! I didn't know you'd seen him."

"He happened to stop by the day the check arrived, and so he rode with me to the bank. That's all."

"Oh, Michael. Do you really believe Jason would steal from you? Is he that desperate?"

"He's not employed, and he didn't look well. He might decide he was stealing from Elizabeth, not from me. Jason could rationalize it that way. And he was always so jealous of her."

Michael was still watching the pigeons. Faith turned away from the table to watch them with him.

"Better Jason than your mother," she said.

Michael didn't say anything, and Faith began to wish that she hadn't, either.

"Is the bank keeping you informed about their investigation?" she finally asked.

"I don't think they're doing much. As far as they're concerned, nobody lost anything. I talked to somebody at the West Hollywood sheriff's station, and he said that Hollywood had jurisdiction, because Max Strother Commodities and the alleged new address are both in Hollywood. He added that it would be a low priority with the LAPD, too, because all I could file a complaint for would be stealing checks and attempted forgery. Even if the person is caught, he or she—and I'm talking about Barbara, Elizabeth's agent, not my mother—even with all our past problems, I really don't think it was my mother—could plead it down to a misdemeanor."

"Then let's investigate it ourselves."

"What?" Michael turned back to Faith.

"I love the way you can express so much disdain for an idea in a single word," she said, uncowed. "Let's check the address and the phone number, at least. We might be able to eliminate both Barbara and Jason, even if we can't do anything more."

"I'd ask if you have a life, but I know you don't. Why do you want to seize my life? Did you make the mistake of calling Brian?"

"No, I heard, though. He and Frances are getting married Sunday. Ten years younger than I am, and she finished her dissertation. She officially gets her Ph.D. Saturday, the day before the wedding. Not that I feel bad anymore about never having finished mine, you know I worked that out. It's been too long since I dropped out of the program, and the family counseling license brings me all the clients I can handle."

Michael nodded and smiled his professional therapist smile. "Well, I suppose neither of us can feel any more inept than we do now, no matter what our next failure is. How do we start our investigation?"

"By calling the phone number, of course. And then driving to the address. Do you have them?"

"The bank gave them to me, to make certain that they weren't mine. They're at my apartment, sitting on my desk. Do we finish our cappuccino first or start our Nick and Nora caper at once?"

"I was thinking more Lord Peter Wimsey and Harriet Vane. Down the cappuccino and let's go." Faith stirred the cinnamon-topped foam into the brew and drank it in two gulps. She didn't like Farmers Market cappuccino very much anyway.

"I don't suppose there was a couple who didn't sleep together." Michael finished his cappuccino and stood, fishing his car keys out of his fanny pack.

"Nancy Drew and Ned Nickerson, but you'll have to wear a football jersey and let me drive."

"Separate cars as far as my place, and then we flip a coin. I'll think about the football jersey."

They threaded their way around tables to the aisle between the falafel stand and the gift shop. That led them to the parking lot, where they parted company.

Faith never liked the hunt for a parking space that she had to endure when she visited Michael's Kings Road condo, so she grabbed the first one she spotted, just north of Santa Monica Boulevard. She walked the block and a half, past buildings that all looked alike—four stories over an underground garage, evenly spaced balconies with views of other balconies, white stucco with greenery around the front doors. Michael was waiting on the sidewalk.

"You might as well have walked from the Farmers Market," he said, unlocking the security door. "There were at least three spaces closer."

"If I owned a Yugo, I could have parked in two of them. The third couldn't accommodate anything bigger than a tricycle."

"Suit yourself, but I could have slid the Honda into all three."

"Then we don't need to flip a coin. When we leave to investigate, you drive, you park."

"Investigate. My God, this is so absurd."

They took the elevator to the third floor. Michael unlocked the deadbolt, and Faith followed him in.

"My God, indeed," Faith said, having held her tongue during the short trip. "It smells like a cattery in here. You ought to show your meal ticket more respect. When did you last change the cat box?"

"Elizabeth doesn't mind the smell. She was born in a cattery, after all. But the cat box is probably still clean. She doesn't like to put her feet in it, so she sort of backs up to it, and sometimes she misses it entirely. Wait here, I'll check."

The cat in question, looking like a blue pearl with darker blue eyes, was stretched out on a pink velvet chair, staring at Faith with what was undeniably attitude.

Michael returned almost immediately, spritzing the air with a pseudo pine scent.

"At least she hit the paper," he said. "I flushed it down, and the smell will be gone in a minute."

"That cat is lucky she's both smart and beautiful, and you don't want to work for a living. It seems to me, though, that if you can teach the cat to give you high fives on camera, you ought to be able to teach her to use the litter, not the paper."

"The difference is, she likes to give high fives on camera."

"The address and the phone number. Quickly. The cat shit smell is not dissipating, and the air freshener is disgusting."

Michael's desk was a rectangle of distressed oak in a corner of his living room. He sat in the bentwood rocker and began sifting through small slips of paper.

"It can't be too far down. I saw it yesterday."

"Why don't you ever file anything?"

"Here it is." He handed Faith an envelope with an address and phone number scribbled on the back. "If I filed, I'd have to clean out the files. I don't have room for files. What I want is on my desk. Everything else I throw out."

"Let's call the phone number."

Michael pointed to the phone. Faith picked it up and punched in the number.

"Four nine two seven," a woman's voice said.

"Michael Haver," Faith responded.

"I can take a message."

"Is that what this is? A service?"

"That's right. What message do you want to leave?"

"Never mind." Faith replaced the phone. "Let's check out the address."

"You know it's going to be a mail drop."

"Yes, but somebody had to establish it. And somebody had to open the trading account, so if we don't find anything out at the mail drop, we talk to Max Strother Commodities."

Elizabeth watched them leave. With attitude.

The La Brea address was indeed a minimall mail drop. Michael parked the Honda right in front.

"It's so simple when you pray to the parking gods," he said.

Faith slammed the car door in answer and marched ahead of him into the narrow store. No one was near the front counter. Both side walls and a center stretch of shelves held boxes, envelopes, tape, and other mailing paraphernalia, carefully arranged to make the selection look larger than it actually was.

"Hello!" Faith called.

A young Asian woman, not more than twenty, emerged from the back.

"Can I help you?" she asked.

"I'm trying to get in touch with Michael Haver. He left this as an address, and I need to talk to him."

"If you leave a message," the young woman said, staring at Faith through large, dark eyes.

"But I don't want to leave a message here. I want to find him."

"You leave a message," the woman repeated.

"This is silly, Fay-ththth," Michael said. "All these places offer confidentiality. That's the appeal."

"Look," Faith said. "This is the real Michael Haver. The Michael Haver who gets mail here is a fake."

"This is Michael Haver? You found him?"

"I know this Michael Haver," Faith said patiently. "I want to find the other one, the one who calls himself Michael Haver but isn't."

"I don't know," the woman answered. "You leave a message, I put it in his box, the Michael Haver box."

"Do you know when he will be in to pick it up?"

"No. Whenever."

"Let's go," Michael said. "Unless you want to leave a message."

"Thank you for your help," Faith said to the woman.

Michael was starting the car before Faith slid into the passenger seat.

"Just one more stop," she pleaded. "Max Strother Commodities. If they can't help, we give up."

"I'm surprised you aren't suggesting a stakeout of the mail drop."

"I thought about it, but there are only the two of us, and I couldn't really count on your cooperation."

"You're right. Max Strother Commodities, and that's it. Where is it?"

"Haven't you ever noticed the sign? It's on the woefully tacky part of Hollywood Boulevard, near Western."

"Dear Lord and Baby Jesus protect us." Michael glared at her briefly, but he turned north on La Brea and east on Hollywood. The neighborhood quickly deteriorated from office buildings to souvenir shops to thrift shops to bars.

Michael parked in a space almost directly in front of the Max Strother Commodities sign, which was on the second story of an Art Deco building too small and probably too deteriorated to make the preservationists' lists. Graffiti almost obliterated the sign warning them of a two-hour parking limit.

"I may wait in the car," Michael said.

"Put the Club on the steering wheel, turn on the alarm, and pray to the antitheft gods," Faith replied.

He caught up with her in the lobby.

The elevator door had an OUT OF ORDER sign. They climbed the stairs, not to the second floor, but to the fourth.

"And you complained about the cat," Michael said as they traversed a landing that smelled of old vomit.

Faith didn't bother to answer.

Max Strother Commodities was at the back of the building, behind a frosted glass-topped door that jangled as they opened it.

"I'll handle this one," Michael added.

The large office was illuminated only by the gray haze from the windows on the back wall. Five-foot partitions had been strategically placed so that visitors couldn't tell how many of the cubicles were actually staffed.

Michael and Faith waited until a short man with a burgundy toupee, wearing a white shirt rolled to the elbows, paisley tie loosened, came to greet them.

"Yeah?" he said.

"I'm Michael Haver." Michael automatically held out his hand.

"The guy who gave us the bum check? No, you aren't."

Michael retracted his hand. "I didn't give you a bum check."

"That's what I said. You aren't the guy."

"Can you describe him?" Faith interjected.

"Who are you?"

"Faith Cassidy, Michael's friend."

"Which Michael? This one or the guy who gave us the bum check?"

"This one. We're trying to find the person who forged Michael's name on the check."

The short man appraised the two of them.

"Got ID?" he asked.

Michael pulled out his wallet and displayed his driver's license.

"The other guy was shorter than you are. Almost bald. Fringe of white hair. Wire-rimmed glasses. Nervous. That's why I remember him. I wasn't surprised when I called the bank and they wouldn't okay the check. Or when the telephone number he gave was a service."

"Oh, hell," Michael whispered.

"You know who it is?" Faith asked.

"Thank you for your time," Michael said.

"No problem."

Faith smiled at the little man, then hurried after Michael.

"Who is it?" she asked again as they started back down the stairs.

"I can't be positive, of course, but the description sounds like Barbara's husband." Michael didn't pause or look back at her.

"Then we have to go see Barbara."

"No. You said Max Strother Commodities would be the end of it. And I want to think before I go any further."

"You have to talk to Barbara—you've known her too long to file a complaint without talking to her—and it seems to me that I ought to be along. Third party."

Michael was moving so quickly that Faith stopped talking. She needed the breath to keep up with him.

A thin young man in a torn t-shirt and jeans was eyeing the Honda when they got to the street. Michael glared fiercely. The young man shrugged and moved away.

"How can I go in and accuse Barbara of stealing from a client?" Michael asked once they were settled, the Club removed from the steering wheel, the engine going.

"You don't accuse her of stealing. You ask her how she's been doing. We approach this as an intervention. We're both licensed therapists, we ought to know how to do this."

"I hope you're right."

Michael took Hollywood Boulevard to Fairfax, then dropped down to Melrose. He parked in front of an art gallery two blocks west.

"Barbara's office is upstairs," he said, as he hit the security buzzer three times in succession. An answering buzz allowed them to open the heavy wood door.

The steps were Spanish tile, the railing wrought iron. The spacious landing had a large fern in front of a window. Another buzzer let them through a second heavy wood door.

"Be right out—I'm on the phone," a voice called.

What should have been a receptionist's office held a mahogany desk cluttered with mail and photographs and a leather couch with more of the same. A signed Frank Romero poster was on the wall.

"Michael darling, what can I do for you?" Barbara swept into the room, a heavy woman in a purple caftan and fringed scarf. "I wish you had called first—I don't have more than a moment."

She presented her cheek to be kissed, and Michael smacked the air next to it.

"Barbara dear, I'm so sorry. This is my friend Faith."

"Oh yes, Fay." Barbara held out her hand. "Michael told me you used to be an actress. So wise of you to change careers—there are so few parts for women your age, and fading ingénues get them all."

Faith smiled. She would have corrected the name, but it didn't feel like the best way to start an intervention.

"I'm just here to listen while you and Michael talk," she said.

"That's fine, I'm sure."

Barbara cleared space for the two of them on the low couch. She perched on the edge of the desk. Faith and Michael looked at each other, then up at Barbara.

"How are you doing?" Michael asked.

"I'm fine, dear, and I don't have time to chat. What is it? Nothing wrong with Elizabeth, is there?"

"Well—not exactly. Almost. Someone tried to steal the bonus from the cat food contract."

"Oh, no. I'm so sorry. Tell me what happened."

Barbara's face wrinkled with concern. Michael and Faith again looked at each other, then up at Barbara.

"Have you ever heard of Max Strother Commodities?" Faith asked, forgetting that she had promised to listen.

"No. Why?"

Michael grabbed Faith's shoulder to keep her from answering.

"Someone forged my signature on a check for twenty-five thousand dollars and tried to open a trading account there. The description sounded a lot like Howard."

"Oh, God. Oh, God." The concern on Barbara's face turned to pain. "Oh, God, don't tell me he did that."

"You knew he had problems?" Faith brushed Michael's hand off.

"Of course I knew. I'm married to him. But I didn't know he'd try to steal from a cat to pay for them." Barbara looked from one to the other. "Howard is a compulsive gambler. He needs help. Would the two of you come with me to talk to him? You're both licensed therapists, you know how to handle this kind of thing."

"We'll do whatever we can to help," Faith cooed.

"Come over for dinner. Seven o'clock. And please, no police."

"You have my word," Michael said, arising from the couch so that he could look Barbara in the eye. "As long as Howard agrees to join a twelve-step program. If he won't go, I file a complaint."

"I'm so grateful." Barbara enveloped Michael in a hug. "This will all work, you'll see."

Faith held out her hand. "Seven o'clock."

She waited until they reached the sidewalk before she said anything more.

"Barbara's lying. She's in it with him."

"How do you know?"

"It was what she said about stealing from the cat. You remember your comment about Jason rationalizing? That's what Barbara did. She wasn't stealing from you, she was stealing from the cat."

Michael considered her words.

"All right. Then she has to join the twelve-step program."

"That's all?"

"And you pay the parking ticket." He plucked it from

the windshield and handed it to her.

"I didn't park in the red zone. But I'll pay if it'll make you feel better."

"Nothing will make me feel better. Not until we've explained to Barbara that attempting to defraud a client is going to cost her the agency franchise. To the Screen Actors Guild, Elizabeth is not just a cat—she's a dues-paying member."

"Michael? Would you rather we hadn't done this?"

"Are you kidding? It's the most effective I've felt since I hit a Little League home run when I was eleven." He kissed her on the cheek. "Now let's go back to my place and plan this intervention. But one stop on the way."

"What?"

"I need to buy a football jersey. And next time, you drive."

Here Today, Dead to Maui

A Faith Cassidy Mystery

I had such a good time writing one short story with Faith Cassidy, her friend Michael, and Michael's cat Elizabeth that when I was asked for a story about cats and vacation, Faith got the nod, even though Freddie O'Neal probably could have used a vacation at that point.

"A millionaire found me changing planes for Maui! Why is he short and ugly, Lord, when you know I like them tall?" Michael sang as he emerged from the bathroom wearing the hibiscus print shirt he had bought the day before.

"That's gross," Faith said. "Materialistic. Midlife Mick Jagger. And nobody came near you on the airplane. Or in the Hilo airport. Except for the fat woman who put the orchids around your neck."

"Because I was traveling with you and Elizabeth. Everyone was looking at her. If I'd been alone, who knows? Besides, if you're so ascetically inclined, why did you accept the offer of a first-class airplane ticket and a week in a suite at the Lahaina Hilton?" Michael leaned against the central post marking the open French doors to the deck and stretched out his arms. "White sand! Ocean! Clean air!"

"Elizabeth's contract specified two tickets. No point in letting one go to waste when you didn't have anybody else to ask." Faith poured herself a second cup of coffee. She didn't particularly like the Kona blend, but it was all room service had to offer.

"Can't you just enjoy the vacation?" Michael turned back and sighed.

"Elizabeth has one more day of shooting. You're not on vacation until tomorrow."

"To Maui, and to Maui, and to Maui. Life creeps in its petty pace, especially when one is not quite on vacation." He knelt down in front of one of the flowered chintz armchairs so that he was level with Elizabeth. "Say *Maui.*"

"Mrowr," she replied, blue eyes focusing intently on his dark ones.

"Maui."

"Mrowr."

"See how smart she is?"

"You didn't feed her this morning. She's actually saying she's annoyed."

Michael straightened up. "When did you become an expert on my cat?"

"I've been part of her environment since you adopted her. She thinks of me as extended family. I felt obliged to return the compliment by paying attention to her behavior. Since I've spent my life—or two careers anyway, the dead one as an actress and the live one as a therapist—studying human behavior, and the cat thinks she's human, it wasn't hard. Trust me. She's hungry."

"So am I." He picked a cheese Danish out of the basket on the coffee table. "But she's supposed to be hungry. Otherwise, she might not eat on cue."

"You'd better hurry with that. Elizabeth's call is in half an hour. Eddie will be here any minute with the car."

"They have to set up a shot on the deck of an old whaler.

No way are they going to be ready on time." Michael poured himself a cup of coffee and settled into the other chintz armchair.

"Then I think you ought to feed her."

"She only has to be hungry and annoyed for the next couple of hours. She'll be fine."

Faith shrugged. "Suit yourself. But if we're going to be here for a while, could you move to another chair? That one clashes with your shirt."

"All the furniture clashes with my shirt. This is Hawaii—the shirt is supposed to clash. Buy a muumuu and get in the spirit."

"Hawaiian clothes are the best thing that could have happened to the tourist industry. You can't tell you've gained fifteen pounds until you're home and it's too late. If I start to gain, I'll think about the muumuu."

"How can anyonc gain on a dict of fish, rice, and fruit? If you're really going to stick to that. Get a muumuu or not. Put orchids in your hair. Drink mai-tais by the pool."

"Maybe when we've finished the shoot." Faith picked a blueberry muffin out of the basket. Blueberries counted as fruit. "I may even search for romance."

"You won't have to search far. Eddie Inouye has made it clear he's available."

"Yes, and he doesn't care who takes him up on the offer. No thanks."

"Well, one of us has to be nice to him if we want him to drive us to the Sacred Pools of Hana tomorrow. The road through the rain forest is supposed to be challenging, and I don't want Elizabeth's life at risk."

"I'll drive," Faith said. "You can hold Elizabeth and look at the scenery."

"I'll have to think about that," Michael replied. He finished his Danish and started on a pecan bun.

"Eddie," they chorused as the phone rang.

Michael stuffed the bun into his mouth and scooped Elizabeth into her carrier. Faith assured Eddie they would be right down.

The elevator took them to the lobby, where Eddie—a short, eager twenty-year-old wearing a shirt that clashed with everything—was waiting.

"Aloha," he said, grinning. "Phil said to tell you they're on time. We have to hurry."

"That has to be a lie. Can I go back for the basket of pastries?"

"I told you we should have fed her," Faith snapped.

"No, no," Eddie said. "He means it. Phil promised he'll have her finished before lunch. Okay?"

"Three hours," Michael said to Faith. "We can handle that."

"Elizabeth is on L.A. time, remember. I've never known you to be this callous."

"Oh, for God's sake, Faith. One morning. For two days' deprivation every six months, she gets to eat shrimp, salmon, and chicken the rest of the year!" Michael turned hastily to Eddie. "Only for snacks, of course. Three meals a day she eats Pretty Kitty cat food."

"Don't worry. Eddie isn't going to turn you in," Faith said. "Are you?"

"No way, *wahine,*" Eddie answered, still grinning. "Driving is my main livelihood. If I talk, nobody wants to ride with me anymore."

Faith nodded. "Let's go."

Eddie had parked his Honda right in front of the hotel, in the taxi loading zone. Two taxi drivers glared as Faith and Michael got into the back seat.

Eddie whisked the car away from the cluster of tall, white hotels, over the causeway, and down the narrow road the short distance to the Lahaina harbor. The day was so beautiful that Faith almost began to enjoy herself.

"What's it like living here?" Michael asked.

"Like this," Eddie answered. "Like every morning when I wake up, it's the first day of vacation."

"It must rain," Faith said. "There's a rain forest on the island."

"Yeah, but it only rains for five minutes at a time. Most of the time. Except for hurricanes, and this isn't the season."

"Stop it, Faith," Michael snapped. "No disasters. I am not anticipating a disaster on Maui."

Faith glared back.

"This is as close as I can get," Eddie said cheerfully. He had maneuvered through the jaywalking tourists to the pier, but there was no place to pull over. Two large silver trucks were taking up three parking spaces apiece. Several horns began to beep the second the Honda's brake lights went on. "I'll find a place to park and meet you on the set. Just yell if you want to make a quick getaway."

"Thanks," Michael said. "I was optimistic enough to schedule a tennis lesson for three and a massage for four."

"No problem." Eddie grinned at him.

The beeps became steady as Faith got out and took Elizabeth's carrier so that Michael could join her. They slipped between the trucks to the wooden walkway.

The whalers were smaller and newer than Faith had expected, but then her idea of a whaler was based on John Huston's *Moby Dick*. She suspected that these had been used since the nineteenth century.

"I don't understand why they're shooting a cat food commercial on a whaler," Faith said.

"Cats love fish," Michael explained, in a tone that let her know any idiot could figure it out. "Pretty Kitty is for cats with a whale of an appetite."

"Yes, but whalers kill whales. When this commercial airs, they're going to lose all the New Agers and Trekkers and Greens who own cats. Maybe half the cat owners in the country." Faith picked her way carefully over heavy cables that snaked from the trucks to a ship halfway down the pier.

"Maybe half the cat owners in L.A., tops. Besides, it's a tax-deductible week in Maui for anyone from Pretty Kitty, the ad agency, or the production company who wants to visit the shoot. Although the L.A. ad business is so bad I don't think anyone from the agency came." Michael waved at the deck. "*Aloha,* we're here."

"Oh, good." A young woman in tank top and jeans leaned over the railing. Two days in Maui had given her Southern California tan a bronze glow and turned the peroxide streaks in her stringy brown hair almost white. She waved a clipboard at them. "Phil is setting up for the shot of Elizabeth now. He's lighting her stand-in."

Michael had one foot on the wooden ladder. He stopped so suddenly that Faith hit him with the carrier.

"What stand-in?" he asked.

The woman held a finger to her lips, then beckoned him aboard.

"What stand-in?" Michael asked again, after reaching the deck in two bounds.

Faith clambered up after him, bracing the carrier awkwardly on each rung.

"Mrowr," Elizabeth said.

"Sorry," Faith murmured to the carrier.

"Faith, Jennifer," Michael said as he belatedly reached for the handle.

"Hi, Faith. Hi, Sweetums," Jennifer added to the carrier.

"Mrowr."

Faith nodded assent.

"Where's Eddie?" Jennifer asked.

"Parking the car. What stand-in?" Michael's voice shot up an octave, and Jennifer shushed him again.

"One of the Pretty Kitty executives is here with his wife, daughter, and cat," she whispered. "The daughter really wants to see her cat in a commercial. I hope Elizabeth is in fine form."

"Of course she is! What an outrage!" Michael snapped.

"Okay, okay," Jennifer said, holding up her hand. "I'm just telling you what's going on."

"We have a contract!" Michael lowered his voice.

"I know. But Pretty Kitty hired the ad agency, and the ad agency hired the production company."

"What does that mean?"

"It means that everyone is being very, very nice. Especially Phil. This is his first network job, you know. I think he'd do anything to get more."

"All right." Michael sighed and turned to Faith. "You see why I didn't feed her. One lousy shot and I'd have to get a job."

"Jennifer! Let's go!" a male voice called.

Faith, Michael, and Elizabeth followed Jennifer aft, stepping between cables when possible.

Cameras, lights, and reflectors were all focused on a very fluffy cat the color of an underripe cantaloupe, wearing a cubic zirconium collar. Her amber eyes darted nervously around the crowd. A red-haired, freckled girl about ten years old was sitting cross-legged beside her, smiling at anyone who would smile back.

"That's Marlene," Jennifer whispered to Michael, drawing the name out to three syllables. "As in Dietrich. The girl's name is Boots. Good luck."

She took the clipboard over to the camera.

Michael shook his head, gaze still fastened on Marlene. "She's pretty, but she's not an actress. We're fine." He looked around, spotting a youth with a three-day growth of beard, whose knees were sticking out of his Levi's. The young man was wearing the only Hawaiian shirt that might have come out of a suitcase, not a store. "Phil! I hope we're not late. I didn't realize we were shooting on MTV video time."

"Hey, Michael, how ya doing?" Phil trotted the four steps that separated them and clapped Michael on the back. "Glad to see the star has arrived." He cupped his hands around his mouth. "Okay! Get ready for a take!" Then he knelt down beside the girl. "Boots, honey. I'm really grateful for your help. And I'm going to remember what a beautiful cat Marlene is, next time we're casting."

Boots looked at him adoringly. She carefully picked up Marlene, then winced when the nervous cat sank bare claws into her naked shoulder.

Michael lifted Elizabeth from the carrier and placed her down on the crossed pieces of silver tape marking the spot Marlene had vacated. Elizabeth stretched, surveyed the assembled group, winked one blue eye at the cameraman, and settled onto her haunches, pearly tail falling naturally into place.

"Here." Someone thrust a crystal dish heaped with Pretty Kitty into Michael's hand. He put it down on another taped mark to Elizabeth's right.

"Roll the tape!" Phil called.

"Rolling!"

"Slate the camera!"

"Slated. Take one."

"Action!"

"Discover the food," Michael whispered.

Elizabeth turned toward the dish. Her eyes widened dramatically. She approached the dish and sniffed, then looked back toward Michael.

"That's right, baby, time to eat," he whispered.

Elizabeth sniffed again. She shook her head. Straightening up, she made a graceful pirouette and overturned the dish with one kick from her left hind leg.

"Cut!" Phil called.

"Oh my God," Michael moaned.

Faith tugged his arm. "There's something wrong with the food."

"What?"

"Something wrong, damn it, *think!*"

"There's something wrong with the food!" Michael yelled.

"What do you mean, son?"

Michael discovered he was standing next to a tall, florid man still decorated with a fading airport lei. Red hair and freckles marked him as Boots's father, even if he wasn't old enough to be Michael's. He was glaring down menacingly.

"I mean sabotage!" Michael gasped. "It can't be Pretty Kitty."

"Come on, Michael." Phil clapped him on the shoulder again. Michael was starting to feel hemmed in. "We'll try another take. If it'll make you happy, we'll even open a new can."

"Where's Elizabeth?" Faith had squeezed between the

men to the overturned dish. Elizabeth was nowhere in sight.

"Elizabeth!" Michael dropped to his knees, to search for her at her own level.

"Hey, guys, anybody seen the cat?" Phil asked.

The murmurs from the crew were all negative.

"Could she have jumped overboard?" The question came from a short, dark-haired woman in a muumuu draped with a fading lei that matched the one Boots's father was wearing.

"Absolutely not!" Michael snapped. Still, he crawled to the edge of the deck and checked the ocean. The gentle, blue waves were unbroken. "Elizabeth!"

His stomach churned, and he began gasping for breath.

"All right! That's enough!" Faith was standing on Elizabeth's mark. The lights had been turned off, but the reflectors focused enough sunlight to create a glow around her shins. Her arms were raised, palms out, like an evangelist. Everyone quieted down and stared. She was glad she hadn't worn a muumuu. The way the long sleeves of her white overblouse fell back past her elbows made a more dramatic effect. "I have to ask one question. You!" Her right hand swooped down, index finger pointing to Boots's father. "Are you driving a rental car?"

"Why, yes." His face became even more florid.

"Thank you." Both palms out again, Faith looked at each silent face in front of her. "I know who took Elizabeth. And I know who sprayed the ant poison on the Pretty Kitty." She waited for the gasps to subside. "We will all turn toward the railing, eyes shut, while I count to thirty. During that time, I expect Elizabeth to reappear on her mark. Otherwise, the person responsible will be looking at both civil and criminal charges. Which will not be good for that person's livelihood. Now! Toward the railing. One! Two!"

Faith had reached twenty-seven by the time she heard the soft *Mrowr* and felt Elizabeth rub against her leg.

"Elizabeth!" Michael cried.

"Thank you all," Faith said, bowing, as the crew applauded.

"Let's get ready for the next take!" Phil shouted. "New can of cat food. Clean up the mess from the old one!"

"I'd like to fix the dish," Faith said.

"Down the stairs to the galley." Phil pointed toward the low cabin.

Michael hugged Elizabeth. He even sobbed a little into her fur, which she didn't like at all.

Faith returned a moment later with the crystal dish, piled high. She set it down on the mark.

Michael released Elizabeth in the general area of the other mark. The cat swiftly groomed the spot where Michael's tears had dampened her fur and then settled precisely in the center of the taped cross, tail flaring gracefully.

"Roll the tape!" Phil called. "Let's do it again!"

Take two went without a hitch. Elizabeth approached the food daintily, then attacked it with gusto.

When she was finished, she sat back and cleaned her face, first with her tongue, then with her paw. The camera captured her entire performance.

"Perfect!" Phil said. "Now the high five!"

Michael prepared for the signature shot that gave Elizabeth her value. He would kneel, with his right arm raised, and snap his fingers. Elizabeth would leap up and slap his palm with her right paw.

This, too, she did perfectly.

"That's a wrap for the cat," Phil said. "Thanks, Michael. Good job."

"You're welcome." Michael had Elizabeth in his arms as

soon as he heard the word *wrap*.

Faith retrieved the carrier from the top of the low cabin, where she had placed it for safekeeping.

"The car's about two blocks away. You want me to get it?" Eddie Inouye materialized next to her.

"I think we can walk back to the hotel," she said. "We want to see a little of Lahaina, and we can do that this afternoon. But tomorrow morning at ten we'd like to leave for some sightseeing, especially the Sacred Pools of Hana. Do you think you could pick us up then?"

"I'll be there." Eddie grinned at her and took off again.

Michael snapped the carrier shut. Jennifer grabbed his arm before he could pick it up.

"I'm so glad Elizabeth is all right," she said. "Really."

Faith had already started down the ladder by the time Michael caught up. He handed her the carrier, then followed her down.

"All right," he said, as they picked their way between cables toward the street. "Which of them was it? Eddie or Jennifer?"

"Both. Eddie sprayed the ant poison, Jennifer grabbed the cat."

"How did you figure it out?"

"Well, I guessed a lot of it. I knew when Eddie said he wouldn't give you away on the cat food that someone else had been talking in his car. It wasn't Marlene's family, because they had a rental. Most members of the crew rode in the trucks with the equipment." She paused until they passed the trucks in question. "And Jennifer pointedly told us that Phil wanted this job to lead to more—not realizing that the best outcome for Phil would be a great commercial, which he wouldn't get if he cast a bad actress in the lead, just to do a favor for the big boss. Favors get more work only at Jennifer's level. Not only that, but from the look on her face when she asked where Eddie was, it occurred to me that he might be a little less available than he was yesterday."

"She enlisted him in the plot?"

"Such as it was. Mostly improvised, I think." They were back on the narrow sidewalk. Faith surveyed the small shops across the street, with their window displays of muumuus. "How about lunch?"

"Tell me the rest first."

"Eddie didn't think we'd suspect ant poison, after you told him that Elizabeth didn't normally eat Pretty Kitty. He thought you'd suspect simple cat perversity."

Michael raised his eyebrows innocently.

"Mrowr," Elizabeth said.

"I know, dear," Faith said to the carrier. "You're a professional. That's the point."

"But when sabotaging the food didn't work, someone had to grab her, someone who knew her, hence Jennifer."

"Good work," Faith said dryly, patting Michael's shoulder.

"How did you know it was ant poison?"

"I didn't. I just thought ants are a problem in tropical climates, so wherever there was food, there had to be ant poison. I checked the galley when I refilled the dish, and I was right."

"I'm awfully glad you're here," Michael said. "I may not always tell you that, but I am grateful for your friendship. I'll buy lunch."

"Here today, dead to Maui," Faith said. "Lunch will do for a start. And did you say you had an appointment for a massage this afternoon?"

"It's yours." Michael sighed.

"Take Elizabeth, run on ahead, and order salmon for three from room service. I'll be there as soon as I've made a quick purchase. Vacation starts now."

"Maui." The word came clearly from the carrier.

"Indeed."

The Fountain Street Ghost

A Faith Cassidy Mystery

This story written for an anthology of stories about Marilyn Monroe was Faith Cassidy's first foray into solving a mystery without a cat.

"If anybody would dream about a visitation from Marilyn Monroe, Bobby would. But I still think holding a séance is a little silly." Faith had to pause for breath. The angle of the Kings Road slope was too steep to climb while talking. "I should have had you drop me off."

"It's only three blocks. That isn't worth taking the car out of the garage for, when I'd just have to put it back in and then walk by myself. You know there's no place to park around here on Friday nights. The overflow from the House of Blues lot takes up everything for miles," Michael responded. "Besides, only this block is uphill. The two blocks along Fountain are flat."

"And then we reach the stairs."

Michael glared and kept walking. Faith hurried to catch up. They had almost reached the end of the block, and Fountain was level, as promised.

Turning the corner didn't change the scenery. Both West Hollywood streets were overbuilt with beige, gray, and white condominiums partially covered with massive shrubbery. The California bungalows that had once graced the area had been deemed an inefficient use of expensive real estate a couple of decades before. Aesthetics loses out to economics every time, Faith thought. She didn't say it because she was conserving her breath for the stairs.

"Bobby thought the apartment was haunted even before the dream about Marilyn Monroe's ghost," Michael said. "And he denies he was asleep. He hired Frankie Fallon to conduct a séance only because he's hoping for confirmation. I don't think that's the least little bit silly. Marilyn did live in the building, after all, which may be the only reason it's still standing. So many people willing to pay premium rent to follow in her footsteps."

"Or whatever," Faith sniffed.

"Is that a polite way of saying that you don't understand the MM mystique?"

"I do understand. Marilyn was a tragic figure, and some disturbed persons find that romantic. I just don't happen to be one of them."

"I hope you're not going to tell Bobby you think he's disturbed."

"Bobby knows very well what I think of him, and my opinion doesn't bother him in the least. I'm sure he also knows that inviting me to a séance confirms it. Why—even if there are ghosts, and I don't believe in them for a minute—why would ghosts talk to Frankie Fallon? Especially the spirits of the stars." Faith stopped at the foot of the stairs leading from the street to Bobby's apartment building. "I'm glad they saved it, for whatever reason. It ought to be a historical monument, if it isn't already."

"I thought you were coming with an open mind."

"I'm doing my best," she sighed, grabbing the railing.

Ornamental urns flanked the steps. The patches of lawn

on either side were neatly trimmed, and the L-shaped stucco chateau beyond seemed newly painted white. White scrollwork outlined the second-story windows, which had been further adorned with tiny round decks and white iron grills. Ivy geraniums mixed with gloxinia spilled between the bars, the red and pink flowers appearing especially bright in the early evening glow. The summer sun wouldn't set for another half hour.

Faith knew they were small decks rather than large window boxes only because she had squeezed onto one of the two off Bobby's living room. Before the high-rise had been built around the corner on La Cienega, the view must have been classic L.A., all the way to Catalina on a clear day.

Another set of stairs inside the building took them up to Bobby's apartment. Faith paused again at the front door.

"The exercise is good for you," Michael said. "You must have put on ten pounds in the last six months."

"Have not," Faith snapped. "I've allowed myself a slight weight gain, but it's been ten pounds spread over a year and two months."

"Spread is the word for it."

"I'm not an actress anymore, and the worth of a therapist isn't judged by her waistline. Fortunately."

"Just what I was going to say." Michael smiled enough to take the sting out of it.

"Are you supporting the cultural imperative?"

"Not at all. I don't think anyone should be judged by appearance, you know that, whether it's Madonna or Sylvester Stallone. Or Marilyn Monroe's ghost, for that matter. And I wouldn't choose either a therapist or a friend based on buffness. As long as you're comfortable and healthy, weigh what you like."

"Thank you." Faith decided not to give him the satisfaction of admitting that sometimes she still worried about how she looked. "That's why so many actresses have eating disorders, you know. They're under so much pressure to stay unnaturally thin that they react by bingeing. One extreme to the other. No sense of moderation. In anything."

The wooden stairs creaked as they climbed.

"How wonderful that changing professions changed your personality. Too bad MM didn't see the light and get out while there was time."

"You're being flippant, but it's true. Getting out of the business—and dealing with the ego problems that come when the attention is gone—has a remarkable effect on one's mental health. At least it was good for mine."

Michael didn't answer. Faith was momentarily annoyed, until she reminded herself that she didn't need his validation.

He lifted the black iron knocker on the apartment door and let it fall.

The burnished oak door was opened almost at once by a young man with shaggy blond hair and a surfer's tan. He wore a brocade vest over a collarless white shirt and jeans, as if undecided about the nature of the occasion he was dressing for. His face was as smooth and bland as a banana-nut muffin.

"Hi, I'm glad you're here." Bobby ushered them into a large, sparsely furnished living room that seemed even emptier because of the cathedral ceiling.

A Swedish modern conversation group that looked straight from the Ikea showroom, complete with striped area rug, faced a white stone fireplace. Michael and Faith each took one of the low chairs.

"Traci called to say that Frankie is running a little late,

but they'll be here. Do you want wine?"

"Yes," Michael said.

"Who's Traci?" Faith asked.

"Traci Sloane. She's Frankie Fallon's assistant. And she drives him everywhere. Don't you watch the show?"

Bobby tossed the question over his shoulder as he headed through the dining alcove to the kitchen. The dining room table had been covered with a white cloth. A brass candelabrum with five white candles waited under the chandelier. The setting sun had glazed the room a soft, rosy pink.

"I don't think I get that channel," Faith called after him.

"It's on channel six," Michael muttered.

"You must tell me the night and time." Faith clasped her hands under her chin and smiled.

"You didn't have to come."

"Yes, I did. I've never been to a séance."

"Here we are, darlings." Bobby set a bamboo tray with a bottle of Chardonnay in an ice bucket and three stemmed glasses on the round coffee table. A plate held a wedge of Brie wreathed with crackers.

"Tell me about your dream," Faith said.

"I wasn't dreaming, I swear it," Bobby answered, handing her a glass. "I was lying in bed, awake, when I heard a woman sobbing. The sound seemed to come from inside the room. And then a blonde in a white halter dress floated through. She glanced over her shoulder, and I saw it was Marilyn."

"Sobbing?" Faith asked.

"Well, no. But the sobbing had stopped by then. For that night, at least. I've heard it several times since."

"Have you checked with your neighbors?"

"Really, Faith. What am I going to do? Start knocking

on strange doors, asking, 'Excuse me, but do you cry in the middle of the night?' " Bobby punctuated the line with his glass, almost spilling the wine.

"You've lived in this building for five years. How can your neighbors be strangers?"

"He didn't say strangers," Michael said. "He said strange."

"I sit corrected." Faith turned back to Bobby. "Don't you know your neighbors?"

"Only by sight. We nod on the stairs, that's all. But even if the sobbing is a neighbor—and if it is, why is it always at three-fifteen in the morning—that doesn't explain the vision." Bobby neatly skinned the top off the Brie and smeared some on a cracker.

"Well, if the vision only appeared once—"

Faith broke off when she heard the door knocker.

"I wasn't dreaming," Bobby said, as he got up to answer it. "And I saw her twice. Then when Frankie Fallon mentioned speaking to Marilyn's spirit on his television show, I simply had to invite him over."

"Hello, dear souls!"

A short, frail man with a halo of wispy red hair swept into the room, followed by a healthy-looking blonde half his age.

Faith and Michael stood while Bobby made the introductions.

"Faith!" Frankie Fallon exclaimed, kissing her hand. "What a wonderful name! Your parents must have had a beautiful vision for their daughter to have named you Faith."

"Thank you," Faith said politely. "I chose the name myself."

She wasn't sure she wanted her hand kissed, but she let

him do it anyway. His skin was so white it was almost translucent, held together by a webbing of blue veins and fine wrinkles. There was so little flesh underneath that Frankie seemed halfway to mummification.

"Even better, dear soul." He looked up at her with large, blue eyes that seemed to be focused on another dimension. "Even better."

As Frankie moved on to inspect Michael, Traci Sloane grasped Faith's hand firmly. Traci's skin seemed especially tanned and solid after Frankie's fragility.

"I'm Frankie's assistant," she said.

Faith wondered if Traci wore all that jewelry on television. The left ear wasn't bad—just a gold half moon with pearl and lapis dangles—but the right ear had a cluster of gold stars hanging from the lobe, plus three small hoops running up the ridge. Three gold chains and a rope of pearls decorated Traci's pink t-shirt. A trendy floral skirt fell almost to her sandals. Faith reminded herself that she wasn't a consultant and kept her mouth shut. She managed a close-lipped smile.

"Would anyone like wine?" Bobby asked.

"No, no, dear soul," Frankie said. "Not until after the séance. Alcohol attracts too many entities, and we may not want them all."

"What does that mean?" Faith asked.

Frankie did his best to focus his blue eyes on them, and Faith found it hard to believe he hadn't consumed the major part of a bottle before he left home.

"Like attracts like," Frankie said. "And spirits attract spirits. That's why so many creative people—actors and writers and artists—become caught by the distilled and fermented kind. They're always surrounded by the ones who have left the flesh, but are still drawn to certain pleasures."

"Are you saying that actors drink because they're surrounded by ghosts who still like the taste?" Faith asked.

"Crudely but wisely put, dear soul." Frankie nodded gently, as if he couldn't remember how to stop. "Creative people are always more sensitive to the presence of the dear departed ones who remain tied to this realm. Many admit that their best ideas come from outside themselves."

Faith sniffed.

Frankie smiled benignly, still nodding. "Although saying these beings remember the taste might be more precise. They can only sense the fumes in their present state. And then there's an amplifier effect, like an echo in reverse. The more one drinks, the more spirits one attracts, and the more spirits one attracts, the more one drinks. Sometimes it becomes hard to remember who is in control. Which is why we will call the spirits before anyone takes another sip of wine."

He held out his arms to gather them in. Traci moved ahead to check out the dining room.

The rosy sun had faded to gray. Traci pulled a lighter out of her shoulder bag and lit the candles.

"A round table would have been better," she said. "Bobby and I can sit on either side of Frankie, but that means Faith and Michael will have to hold hands across the table."

"And we will all do that," Frankie said, "as soon as we have washed our hands. I want a clean connection."

"The bathroom is down the hall to the left," Bobby said. "But it'll be quicker if those who don't have to use the facility for other purposes wash in the kitchen."

Faith took the kitchen. She wanted to stay as close as possible to the dining room. Since Traci used the kitchen sink as well, she was able at least to keep her in sight. Faith began to wish she had inspected the table when she first arrived. But she didn't really think Bobby would rig a séance for her benefit, and neither Traci nor Frankie was left alone in the dining room.

Faith was reasonably confident that nothing would happen when the others returned to the dining room.

They sat as Traci had directed, Frankie at the head of the table, with his back to the kitchen, Traci and Michael on one side, Bobby and Faith on the other.

"Take hands, dear souls," Frankie said, reaching for Traci and Bobby. "And shut your eyes."

Faith felt awkward, stretching her arm across the table for Michael's hand, but she managed. She didn't like shutting her eyes—that was giving an opening for someone to set something up—but she did as told.

The soft, clean hands in hers seemed to form a water seal, bonding her to the circle.

"We ask for a cone of white light," Frankie said. "We ask that only spirits of goodwill come within this room. We would like to speak particularly with the entity who was once known as Marilyn Monroe. Give us a sign when you're here, dear soul."

Faith opened her eyes to slits and tilted her head to check the others. Everyone was sitting with head bowed and eyes closed, presumably holding hands.

A faint breeze wafted across the room. Faith saw the candles flicker. She struggled against a rush of anxiety, but it faded as the flames steadied. Michael's eyes popped open.

"Thank you, dear soul," Frankie said. "You can all open your eyes now, or leave them closed, as you wish."

Traci and Bobby opened their eyes. Frankie stayed with his head bowed a moment longer.

"I have the spirit of Hedda Hopper," he said, finally

opening his eyes. "She wants us to know that Marilyn won't be coming tonight because there is someone in this room who doesn't adore her. Marilyn didn't like to attend gatherings where one person didn't adore her when she was still in the flesh, and she sees no reason why she should do so now."

"Oh, God, Faith," Bobby moaned. "I knew I shouldn't have invited you."

"I can leave," Faith snapped.

"No, no, dear soul," Frankie said. "The circle is formed. Hedda can tell us everything we need to know."

"Has Marilyn been here?" Bobby asked.

"Yes, dear soul. Hedda says that Marilyn's spirit has indeed visited this building where she once lived."

"Does she want something from me?"

Frankie was silent. Faith was annoyed to realize that they were all trying to hear whatever Frankie listened for.

"Hedda says that Marilyn's visits do not concern you directly, although she is pleased that you cared enough to invite this humble channel." Frankie was staring at a spot on the far wall of the living room. Faith fought the urge to turn around to check for ghosts.

"Is she here for the crying woman?" Bobby asked.

"Hedda believes so, but she says she has no information on that entity."

"Why not?" Faith asked.

Bobby glared at her.

"Some things are not revealed to us, dear soul," Frankie said. "But Hedda does have a message for you. She says your grandmother Myrtle, who wanted to be an actress in life, is enjoying the company of many from the Hollywood community now that she has passed on. Burt Lancaster is especially fond of her, and Myrtle is happier than she dreamed possible."

"What?" Faith was so startled that she would have dropped hands if Bobby and Michael hadn't held firmly.

Frankie ignored her. "Myrtle is pleased that you pursued her dream even though it didn't quite work out as you wanted, and she hopes that your new career will be rewarding. She says you will have a new client soon."

Faith was too stunned to respond.

"Does Hedda have a message for me?" Bobby asked.

"Yes. Marilyn is so pleased with you that someday, when you need a prayer answered, she will see that it is granted."

"Wow!"

Faith kept her grip on Bobby's hand.

"Hedda has another message for one in our circle," Frankie said.

"I hope this one is mine," Michael said.

"Yes, dear soul. The message is from your grandfather, Thomas. Thomas knows that the Lord takes care of the lilies of the field, and will surely provide for you, but he nevertheless wishes you would devote more time to your psychotherapy practice. He reminds you that you have gifts that are needed by others, and he hopes you will make use of them."

"At least that was good advice," Faith muttered.

"Hedda has one last message for the company, this one from James Dean. He says you are all very talented people with the potential for great success, as long as you don't drink and drive."

"More good advice," Michael whispered.

The candles flickered in a new breeze.

"Another spirit wishes to speak with us. Jean Harlow says that she does have information about the crying woman." Frankie nodded at something in whatever unearthly realm his eyes were focused on.

"How did Jean Harlow get into this?" Faith muttered.

"Jean Harlow felt a kinship with Marilyn, and occasionally checked on her while she was living here. She still maintains some contact with the building because she finds it so entertaining," Frankie answered. "Jean says the woman is married to a musician, and the reason she starts crying at three-fifteen is that if he isn't home by then, he isn't coming at all."

"That makes sense," Bobby said. "Although crying about it isn't going to do her any good."

"Why doesn't she just leave him?" Michael asked.

"Jean says it's a karmic tie from a past life, and the woman isn't able to change the pattern without help. She says that's why Marilyn has allowed herself to be seen in this building, to draw attention to the situation and get help for the woman. Marilyn hopes one of you will interfere."

"That's for you, Faith," Bobby whispered.

"Why does Marilyn care?" Faith asked.

"Hedda says that Marilyn is improving her chances for a happier incarnation next time by doing occasional good deeds while her soul is in energy form. This crying woman is one of her projects."

"Celestial community service?" Michael asked.

Everyone ignored him.

The candles flickered one more time.

"Hedda says goodbye for now. And so does Jean." Frankie continued to stare in the general direction of the living room wall a moment longer, then blinked and smiled at each of them in turn. "Are you happy, dear souls? You can break the circle if you wish."

"Thrilled," Bobby replied. "Would anyone like wine now? Except Traci, who's driving."

"We would love to spend some time with you, dear souls, but we have another engagement this evening,"

Frankie said, patting Bobby's hand with the one that had been holding Traci's.

"Don't blow the candles out," Traci said. She stood up and rearranged her shoulder bag. "Let them burn to the stub if you can, otherwise snuff them."

"I'm so grateful," Bobby said, dropping Faith's hand to double the clasp with Frankie. "I hope we can do this again."

"Any time, dear soul, any time."

Faith and Michael stayed in their seats as Bobby showed the medium and his assistant to the front door.

"Well?" Michael asked.

"I'm sure it's all explainable," Faith answered.

"Then explain it out here," Bobby called from the living room. "And don't blow the candles out."

Faith was tempted, but she refrained.

"Didn't you have to pay him?" she asked, after they had regrouped by the fireplace.

"Credit card over the phone when I made the appointment," Bobby said.

"If he's such a good psychic, you'd think he could sense the deadbeats," Faith said.

Michael tried to shush her, and Faith regretted the comment. A true psychic would indeed ask Bobby for a credit card in advance.

"How would you explain the breeze?" Bobby asked, ignoring the comment.

Faith took a sip of wine. It was a little too warm, but drinkable. "Some kind of air pump in that shoulder bag, triggered by Traci's foot under the table."

"And the names? I gather you have a grandmother named Myrtle."

"He could have gotten my grandmother's name from records somewhere. Everything's on the Internet now."

"Everything but why the woman cries," Bobby replied. "I don't know why you have to tear down the curtain, Faith. Why can't you just accept that we aren't in Kansas anymore?"

"Where's Kansas?" Michael asked.

Both Faith and Bobby glared, and he shrugged his shoulders.

"Sorry," he added.

"Wherever we are, I don't believe ghosts are hanging around to give us advice," Faith said.

"Then I think you should stay the night." Bobby stated it firmly, punctuating again with his wine glass. He licked off the few drops that fell on his wrist.

"What?"

"Oh, for God's sake, Faith, that isn't a proposition. You can sleep wherever you like, as long as it isn't with me. But I think you should find out for yourself what's going on," Bobby said.

"I agree." Michael nodded, clearly enjoying the situation. "I think you should stay and find out for yourself. After all, Jean Harlow said Marilyn wanted someone to interfere."

"Frankie said, you mean," Faith said, ready to argue.

"Frankie said Jean said Marilyn said," Bobby chanted.

"Faith, you know you want to," Michael said.

By the time the bottle of wine was gone, Faith had decided they were right.

"I'll stay out here, in one of the chairs," she said. "I don't want to fall into a sound sleep. I want to be alert."

"Call me tomorrow and let me know what happens," Michael said, kissing her on the cheek.

"I may have to call sooner than that—my car is in your garage."

"Take a cab home if it's before ten. We'll have lunch, and I'll get you back to your car."

Bobby saw him to the door.

"You don't have to amuse me," Faith said when he returned.

"I'm just picking up the glasses," he replied. "And then I'm going to snuff the candles. I have Tetris on my Nintendo, if you want to amuse yourself."

"Do you have a book?"

"I have a week's worth of the trades, plus the current *Dramalogue*."

Faith shook her head. "I don't do that anymore. I'll just sit here and brood until morning."

"Suit yourself."

Once Bobby had gone to bed and the lights were out, Faith understood how the apartment could inspire visions of ghosts. Pale light from the high windows cast shifting shadows on the walls.

If there is a ghost, she thought, it ought to be Peter Cushing's.

But it was Marilyn Monroe who danced at the periphery of her mind, just out of reach. Faith was wide awake, certainly, when she tried to focus on the haze in the corner, inches beyond the moonglow. How sad she felt, how sad that she couldn't quite see.

She almost jumped out of her skin when a hand touched her shoulder.

"I thought you weren't going to sleep," Bobby said.

"I wasn't asleep."

"You were. I had to shake you. You haven't heard the crying, have you?"

"What—" Faith started, then stopped. She hadn't heard it consciously, but that had been the source of her own feeling of sadness. The sobbing.

As she listened, the low sobbing crescendoed to a high wail, filling the room.

"It must be the woman downstairs," Bobby said. "I've tried to figure out where the sound is coming from, and it has to be rising through the heat vents."

"Well, time to meddle."

"Are you sure you want to?"

"No, but I think someone should. If I were crying like that, I'd want someone to help me. And so I guess I have to try to help her." Faith struggled out of the chair and stretched her stiff legs.

"Your grandmother said you were going to have a new client soon."

"Frankie said that. And it was a safe prediction, since he didn't say how soon."

"Well, good luck. I'll be waiting."

Faith ran her hand through her hair and thought about a mirror and some fresh makeup, but a new wail set her moving toward the door.

The hall was quiet and dimly lit. Faith moved quickly down the stairs.

She leaned her ear against the door directly below Bobby's and thought she could discern muffled sobs. She rapped the iron knocker sharply, and the sound stopped. While she was trying to decide whether to keep knocking or leave, the door opened a crack, held by a chain.

Faith caught a glimpse of a single puffy eye, and then the door slammed shut.

She lifted the knocker and let it fall one more time.

"I thought you might want to talk," she called.

She had started back down the hall when a woman's voice stopped her.

"Wait—don't leave yet."

The woman standing in the doorway had the anguished look of an abandoned child. Dark hair hung limply around a red, swollen face. She hugged a stained flannel bathrobe close to her thin body.

"I'm sorry," she said. "For a minute I thought you were Marilyn's ghost. But you're too old, and your hair isn't blond enough, and she never appears in her frumpy period, the way she looked when she was married to Arthur Miller. I guess you have to be real."

"Marilyn's ghost?" Faith was too stunned to comment on the rest of the woman's reaction to her.

"Yes. I've seen her several times. She lived in this building, a long time ago."

"I know Marilyn lived here." Faith stared at the woman, not certain how to continue.

"What did you want?"

"A friend of mine lives upstairs. We heard you crying, and I thought you might want to talk. I'm a therapist."

The woman wiped her eyes with one hand, then looked at Faith again. "Maybe I do want to talk. I don't know." She shivered for a moment. "Not now. Do you have a card or something?"

"Upstairs. I left my purse upstairs."

"Stick the card through the mail slot. Maybe I'll call you."

Faith was trying to think of something more to say when the woman shut the door.

Bobby had kept his promise to wait up. He even fixed Faith a cup of tea while she called a taxi. She told him briefly what had happened.

"Do you think you'll hear from her?" he asked.

"I'll have to wait and see," she answered.

By the time she met Michael for lunch the next day, Faith had more information.

The woman had already made an appointment to talk.

"Why did she decide to trust you?" Michael asked.

"She had asked Marilyn's ghost for help, and for a moment she thought I was Marilyn's ghost, answering her prayer. Then she realized I don't look much like Marilyn Monroe." Faith decided not to mention the word frumpy. "She still thinks Marilyn's ghost answered her prayer."

"Are you ready to revise your opinion of Frankie Fallon yet?"

"Not really. I asked Lily—that's the woman's name—if she had ever heard of him, and it seems that she had called him one night after hearing him mention Marilyn's spirit on his television show. Probably the same one Bobby saw. She told Frankie that she was praying to Marilyn's ghost." Faith put on her glasses to study the menu, but she could feel Michael staring at her.

"Are you suggesting that Frankie Fallon set all this up to make it appear as if Marilyn Monroe's ghost was answering Lily's prayer?"

"I think it's possible."

Michael put his hand on the menu, so she had to glance up at him over the top of her glasses.

"If you're truly convinced he's a bad wizard, then you have to admit he's an awfully good man, at least when it comes to providing for the lilies of the field."

"Your grandfather mentioned them."

"Frankie mentioned them."

"I remember. Let's eat."

"And the ghost?"

"Maybe it wasn't a ghost." Faith gently removed his hand. "Maybe it was an angel. Who knows?"

AFTERWORD

I heard that Marilyn Monroe was dead on Sunday afternoon. A friend called me, crying, to pass on the news that Marilyn Monroe had committed suicide the night before. I was stunned and puzzled and, at least to some extent, despairing. If Marilyn Monroe couldn't find love and happiness, what hope was there for the rest of us?

I was living in New York that year, studying acting at Neighborhood Playhouse. I thought Marilyn was funny and charming and sexy, and if she wasn't taken seriously as an actress, well, so what? Neither was anyone else except for Katharine Hepburn and a few old Brits. I envied her fame—especially when it brought her the opportunity to sing "Happy Birthday" to President Kennedy. (I didn't envy Jackie Kennedy. And I still have trouble believing that only people in the entertainment industry knew of her husband's escapades.) I wondered what it would be like to be Marilyn Monroe, and still to fall victim to the dark night of the soul.

Since then, she has become my own private metaphor to describe the difficulties that uncommon women have in maintaining relationships: Marilyn Monroe was home alone on a Saturday night when she killed herself. (Where have you gone, Joe DiMaggio?) Arguments that she wasn't really alone or that her suicide might have been abetted only beg the question. Marilyn Monroe had no "significant other." And who were we women in 1962 unless we were with men?

With that in mind . . . what would Marilyn's ghost be doing today?

Cat, the Jury

A Faith Cassidy Mystery

I received the invitation to write a story for an anthology about cats and courts not long after I had moved to Ventura. I couldn't resist dragging Faith Cassidy there, if only for the afternoon. Around the time I finished the story, I ran into Michael Collins at a party and asked for his professional opinion on titles—should I call it "Cat, the Jury" or "Reasonable Doubt"?

" 'Cat, the Jury'—'I, the Jury' with a cat?" Michael gasped, then recovered. "Everybody has written a story called 'Reasonable Doubt.' Call it 'Cat, the Jury.' " So I did.

"If there ever was an excuse to get out of jury duty, this is it. Show me the notice again."

"Wait till we get to our table." Michael headed purposefully toward the one vacant table near the small lunch counter and grill.

Two burly, bearded men wearing Harley Davidson vests above their swimming trunks glared as Michael cut them off. He pretended not to notice.

"We shouldn't have come to the beach." Faith stopped, ready to retreat, but the two men moved away without comment.

"Of course we should have come," Michael replied. "Although next time we're going to rent one of those tables with the yellow umbrellas."

"Making reservations for the beach seems un-American. Still . . ." Faith let the sentence trail away. If the bikers had wanted to argue, they would be eating sand with their sandwiches.

The August heat had rendered West Hollywood uninhabitable. When Michael had called that morning asking Faith to cancel whatever appointments she had and join him in a trip to the beach, Faith had confessed that the two clients scheduled for the afternoon had already cancelled. She lived in an older building, with only a window unit to cool her combination office and living room, and one client had explained politely that suffocating heat was not conducive to productive psychotherapy. The other had left a message on her answering machine while she was in the shower.

Michael had read about a European-style area of the Ventura beach where yellow umbrellas had been set up near a small espresso and sandwich bar, allowing spur of the moment beach-going and instant picnics. Ventura sounded like a long drive for nothing to Faith, but since Michael was driving, she agreed to go.

Once they had walked the length of the rickety old Ventura pier and back, stopping to watch the group of fishermen at the end, she was too tired and hungry to walk down the beach to the yellow umbrellas. The lunch counter on the pier was as far as she was willing to move. Besides, the area with yellow umbrellas was packed with escapees from the city. They hadn't thought to make reservations, so they would have had to wait.

The topper was that she was almost cold. Not quite, but almost. The Los Angeles basin was well over a hundred degrees when they left. The Ventura beach wasn't even eighty, and there was a stiff breeze from the ocean. With just a light terrycloth jacket over her bathing suit, Faith wanted shelter. The pier provided it, the beach didn't.

Still, she had to admit that the Ventura beach had its charms, with its clear green water and slightly hazy blue sky. The ocean ended not at the horizon, but in an offshore mist that hid the Channel Islands from view. That was why the breeze was so cool—the marine layer.

Faith set the plate with her grilled veggie burger on the small table next to Michael's teriyaki *ahi* sandwich. She took a long swallow of her iced tea.

"Elizabeth is a cat," she said. "A cat can't be a juror. How did they get her name?"

"From the voter registration rolls. I bet Bobby that the system was so lax that I could register Elizabeth and no one would check. I was right. And so Elizabeth—my cat—has been summoned to jury duty."

Faith examined the summons. Municipal Court in Van Nuys. She took a bite of her veggie burger and thought about the heat. The pervasive heat, the heat that she had been wandering through malls and going to afternoon movies to get away from. The heat that they had come to the beach to escape. The heat that would be waiting for her when she returned to the city, returned to an apartment with only a fan in the bedroom and a window unit in the combination office/living room for an air conditioner.

"I'll go," she said.

"My God! Why?"

"The courthouse will be cooler than my apartment—anything would be—and all my clients are canceling until the end of the heat wave. I don't blame them, either. I might as well do something useful. They have an on-call system, so I don't have to go every morning. And it's for

Municipal Court. That means even if I get a trial, it'll be somebody fighting a traffic violation, or petty theft, or a minor dope bust, something like that. It'll only take a few hours. I'll take a book with me and read in the jury room the rest of the time. Elizabeth will have done her civic duty and no one will know you diddled with the political system."

"What will you use for identification? I didn't get her a driver's license, and you don't look like a six-year-old blue-point Himalayan anyway."

"The last time I was a juror no one checked for identification. I showed up with a badge and they took my word for it. People try to get out. They don't try to get in. If you're worried, ask Bobby to make me a driver's license. He can get something out of his computer that I could flash in a pinch."

"That's breaking the law," Michael pointed out.

Faith rolled her eyes and took another sip of her iced tea.

"I'll only have to lie about my name. The rest of it is close enough. Elizabeth is a television actress—television commercials are the art form of the new generation—and I used to be a television actress. Would you rather explain why Elizabeth can't be a juror?"

"I'll get you something that will pass."

Faith nodded. She picked up her veggie burger and prepared to enjoy the rest of the afternoon.

When the alarm went off on Monday morning, Faith awoke with a jerk that scattered Amy and Mac, her two domestic longhairs, from the bed. It took a few startled, puzzled seconds for her to remember why she had set it the night before.

"Jury duty," she muttered.

Mac stared at her, wild-eyed.

"It's for Elizabeth," she explained. "Michael's cat. A long story."

Amy headed for the kitchen, certain food would be forthcoming soon.

And Faith headed for the shower, not certain that it was going to do much good. The day was going to be another scorcher.

Even getting dressed and made-up required taking breaks in front of the wheezing window unit. She was damp before she left the building. With a book under her arm and a jacket over it, in case the courthouse was actually refrigerated, she dashed for her car, the one place in the world where the temperature was under her control.

Surely, jury duty would be better than another day in the heat.

She took Coldwater Canyon over the hill, past Ventura Boulevard and on to Victory Boulevard, where she turned left toward the government complex that included two courthouses, one Municipal, one Superior. Following the directions on Elizabeth's summons, she found the jury parking lot. A young man glanced at the card and waved her through. He had waved at the car before, and he waved at the car after.

The new jurors were all arriving at the same time—and the line of cars moving slowly into the structure meant that they would all be late.

Faith parked between the two cars that had been with her coming in. She fell into step with the fiftyish man in a work shirt and jeans who emerged from one and the sixtyish woman in a cotton blouse and skirt who emerged from the other as all three walked briskly across the street and right, toward the building that housed the Municipal Court.

There was another bottleneck just inside the door. Everyone had to pass through the metal detector. Nobody set it off, and the guard seemed bored.

The herd moved as one to the jury room. Faith sat and waited for her name—Elizabeth's name, that is—to be called. Whoever had summoned them all clearly had done this before and knew they would all be late. The public address system came to life about half an hour after she arrived.

Faith sat and waited through the orientation, first listening to a clerk explain the routine, then watching a videotaped judge explain the system. She sat and waited through a long silence. The room felt uncomfortably like a bus terminal, and she didn't really feel like reading the paperback novel she had brought. But at least it was cool. And not too cold.

Shortly before noon, the speakers came to life again, and an amplified voice called out, "Municipal Court will not be seating a jury today. Superior Court, however, needs jurors. At one thirty, the following prospective jurors will report for duty at the Superior Court building on the other side of the walkway. If your name is not called, you are dismissed for the day. Walter Ivey, Jane Guerin, Elizabeth Haver . . ."

Faith was picking up her things, getting ready to leave, when she realized unhappily that she was now Elizabeth Haver.

The voice gave directions to the courtroom.

As ordered, Faith reported to the Superior Court building after lunching in the crowded cafeteria. No one wanted to leave the area. It would have meant exposure to the heat.

The man and woman she had met in the parking structure were among the group in the hall waiting for the courtroom door to open.

"Bad luck," the woman said brightly, nodding at Faith. The woman had short white hair and wore heavy bifocals that reflected the light from the windows.

Faith nodded in return. She didn't really want to get caught in small talk. It would mean establishing her identity as Elizabeth Haver, and she wanted to keep the lies to a minimum.

It was almost two when the bailiff opened the door and motioned them all inside.

More waiting, more listening to instructions.

And it dawned on Faith as the first twelve prospective jurors were questioned that if she were seated, and if she told them her name was Elizabeth Haver, she wouldn't simply be lying. She would be committing perjury—actually breaking the law. She thought about explaining to the bailiff that this was all a mistake, that she had to leave. She thought about suddenly becoming ill.

She imagined the cold eyes of the judge penetrating her heart.

There was no easy out, no way she could tell the truth without making things worse. Perjury it would have to be.

She tried to figure out from the questions what kind of crime the defendant was charged with. It had to be violent, and serious, or the judge wouldn't care so much which of the prospective jurors had recently been victimized.

The defendant was a woman, a grossly obese woman with a spiky halo of flaming red hair. She didn't look particularly violent, although she did look vaguely familiar. Faith had seen her face before. On television. She remembered the protruding blue eyes with the dark shadows beneath.

The *voir dire* questions that weren't about crime all seemed to do with belief in extrasensory perception.

The prosecutor was using his peremptory challenges to get rid of jurors who absolutely believed in psychic phenomena. The defense attorney was using hers to get rid of skeptics.

The judge was excusing people who said they had seen so much media coverage of the case that their minds were made up.

Faith remembered who the woman was. Molly Jupiter, billed as the World's Greatest Psychic. A few months earlier she had been arrested for the murder of Charles Bennis, operator of a psychic hotline that was advertised extensively on late-night television. Faith hadn't paid too much attention to the media coverage because too much had been happening in her own life at the time. All she remembered was the fat psychic, who had seemed even fatter on television, refusing to talk.

If Faith wanted to avoid this jury, all she had to do was tell them her mind was closed, one way or the other. Closed on psychic phenomena, certain the woman was a murderess.

Unfortunately, her mind was open on both. It was one thing to lie about her name, another to lie about her tolerance and sense of fair play.

At the end of the afternoon, Faith—now Elizabeth Haver—was one of twelve jurors sworn in to decide the case of Molly Jupiter.

Opening arguments were scheduled for ten the following morning.

Faith glumly trudged out of the courtroom.

The white-haired woman, also on the jury, caught her at the escalator.

"What do you think?" she asked. "By the way, my name is Jane."

"I think we shouldn't discuss it," Faith said. "And my name is—Elizabeth."

"Glad to meet you. You mentioned when the judge was asking questions that you're an actress. Might I have seen you in anything? You do look familiar." Jane seemed determined to strike up a conversation.

"Uh, no, I don't think so. I've been living on residuals, nothing recent."

Faith was almost glad to hit the heat. Walking from the courthouse to the parking structure left both women short of breath, ending all talk.

They waved goodbye as they reached their cars.

Turning the air conditioner to maximum cool restored Faith's good humor. She considered driving until morning, until it was time to return to court.

She went home because her cats were there. And she needed to confess her crime to Michael.

"Faith, you knew it would be perjury," he said when she called.

"I didn't think. Could I be prosecuted?"

"I don't know. Probably not—or at least not unless you cause a mistrial. Are you sure you want to go ahead?"

"Forward is easier than back."

"And it's in a good cause."

"I know. You read about all these lousy court decisions. Maybe I can do something right."

"Don't flatter yourself. The cause is staying out of the heat, and you know it."

Faith sniffed. "Partly true. Besides, I want to know what happened. This was a case that got some attention. I'll tell you about it just as soon as I can."

"Of course. You don't want to add misconduct to perjury."

"That's enough. I'll call you tomorrow."

The bottleneck at the door to the Superior Court building reached all the way down the stairs. Faith was perspiring heavily by the time the guards passed her through the metal detector. And not in a good mood.

"Elizabeth!"

A hand tapped Faith's shoulder. Startled, she turned to see the juror named Jane, smiling at her.

"I was thinking about you last night," the older woman said. "What good experience this will be, if you're ever cast in a crime series."

Faith made a weak attempt to smile back.

"I suspect it isn't the same," she said, moving purposefully toward the escalator.

Jane scurried to catch up. "Well, we'll certainly find out, won't we?"

The crowd had thinned in the hall, but the escalator renewed the bottleneck.

Faith realized that she would be doomed to chat with Jane for the duration of the trial. She turned, calling on all her reserves of charm, and found a smile that was almost sincere.

"Yes, we surely will," she said.

She smiled through the wait in the hallway, smiled as the bailiff called them in, smiled as Jane kept talking.

Once seated in her spot as Juror Number Four, Faith began to study Molly Jupiter, who was having a whispered conversation with her attorney.

The woman could have gone straight from the courtroom to the Renaissance Fair. She was wearing several layers of dark blue cotton, including a blouse, a long ruffled skirt, and an equally long sleeveless vest. Her pudgy hands were clasped in front of her in a manner that seemed to Faith too relaxed for the circumstances. She searched for signs of tension.

As if sensing Faith's attention, the woman glanced at her, focused the protruding eyes for a moment, eyes that seemed even a deeper blue this morning, nodded, and returned to her conversation. The attorney, whose beige tailored suit offered a striking contrast to her client's dress, didn't seem to notice the shift in attention.

"All rise," the bailiff called.

The judge, a dark-haired woman with a friendly face, entered and took her place. She greeted the jurors, called for the opening arguments, and the trial was underway.

The prosecutor was a young black man who looked barely out of law school.

"Ladies and gentlemen of the jury," he began, looking each of them in the eyes, one at a time. "The defendant is charged with brutally murdering her former employer, a man who had built her professional career. Because of the nature of the crime, I will have to describe acts and show photographs that will offend some of you. Let me apologize in advance. But there is no other way."

The prosecutor proceeded to tell them how Charles Bennis had advertised in several magazines catering to those with an interest in the occult, looking for someone who could be billed as the World's Greatest Psychic. He auditioned close to a hundred psychics before hiring Molly Jupiter.

Bennis set her up as star of her own psychic hotline, complete with infomercials on late night cable. The money poured in. Then Molly Jupiter decided she wanted to be in business for herself. Bennis threatened to sue. He was bludgeoned to death two days later.

A piece of skin matching Molly Jupiter's DNA was found under Bennis's fingernails, the defendant had a scratch on her arm, and she had no alibi for the time of the murder.

"Circumstantial evidence, yes," the prosecutor said. "But circumstantial evidence can be convincing. Think of the light inside your refrigerator. How do you know it goes out when you close the door? Can you see it? No. You know there is a light switch, and you believe that the door hits the light switch when it closes, and the light goes out. Circumstantial evidence. But you have no doubt that the light goes out."

Molly Jupiter sat quietly, looking at her hands, as the prosecutor dramatized the story. Faith wondered again if she were truly that calm, even as the prosecutor had the jury seeing the fat woman as a murderous refrigerator door.

The defense attorney's statement was short.

"Much of what you have heard is true," she said. "One thing is not. Molly Jupiter did not commit the murder. This is a case of mistaken identity. The police arrested the wrong psychic. The real perpetrator was not Molly Jupiter but her cousin, Melinda Parris, who was passed over originally for the title of World's Greatest Psychic, and then passed over a second time, when Molly left the hotline. Molly Jupiter was framed. What you will hear is circumstantial evidence. Nothing places Molly Jupiter at the crime because she wasn't there. Someone cut off the victim's light. But it wasn't Molly Jupiter."

The defense attorney looked each of them in the eyes, just as her counterpart had previously.

Reasonable doubt, Faith thought. All she has to do is convince one of us that there is a reasonable doubt. A case of mistaken refrigerator doors.

At the end of the opening statements, the judge ordered a lunch break.

"Do you mind if I join you, Elizabeth?"

"Not at all, Jane." Faith sighed. It was going to be a long trial.

The assistant district attorney took four days to present his case. First he established a motive, calling several witnesses to testify that Molly Jupiter had been struggling to survive when she had answered the ad, that Charles Bennis had saved her from certain bankruptcy, and that there had been loud, ugly arguments when she wanted to leave the hotline and go out on her own. Two psychics who worked the hotline confirmed that threats on both sides escalated when Bennis said he would sue Jupiter for everything she was worth if she started a competing service.

During cross-examination, both psychics admitted that they had trouble imagining Molly Jupiter as a murderess.

Then the assistant district attorney called the coroner and showed the promised photographs of the bludgeoned body. He was right. They were ugly. Faith was more disturbed by them than she had expected to be.

There was also a photograph of Molly Jupiter's arm, showing what appeared to be a partly healed scratch.

The circumstantial evidence tying Molly Jupiter to the crime scene was mostly built around the DNA. When cross-examined, the DNA expert had to admit that sometimes first cousins were genetically close enough to confuse the issue. No one had checked Melinda Parris's DNA.

There was a lot of hypothesizing about Jupiter going to Bennis's house on the pretext of settling differences, most of which the defense attorney objected to and the jury was told to ignore.

The defense attorney had her turn the following Monday morning.

She called Melinda Parris to the stand.

The cousins certainly looked alike. Melinda Parris was as round as Molly Jupiter, with the same protruding eyes, although she had spiky black hair and dressed in layers of white cotton. Faith wondered about the choice. It made her think of refrigerator doors again.

The testimony was short. Melinda Parris denied committing the murder.

"I had no motive," she insisted. "I was in a position to take over the hotline. In fact, if you check the phone records, you'll see that I was signed on to the computer that evening, taking calls. I have an alibi."

"One of those calls was well over an hour," the defense attorney pointed out. "You could have faked the call to yourself, which would have given you plenty of time to commit the murder."

Melinda Parris rolled her eyes. "But I didn't."

That was the entire defense. Molly Jupiter didn't take the stand.

The closing arguments were much the same as the opening ones.

The judge instructed the jury to decide whether Molly Jupiter was guilty beyond a reasonable doubt.

Faith looked again at Molly Jupiter. The woman responded to Faith's gaze almost as she had at the beginning of the trial. But this time as she met Faith's eyes, she seemed to mouth the word "meow" before she turned away.

"Remarkable," Michael said as he refilled Faith's wine

glass. "But you probably imagined it."

They were sitting on Michael's deck. The late afternoon sun was obscured by smog, but the worst of the heat wave had passed.

"Of course. That's what I thought, too. Still, I had a sense of a meeting of the minds. As if she knew what I had done, that I had assumed a cat's identity, and knew at the same time that I wasn't a criminal. I believed that she was a victim of mistaken identity. And I couldn't believe the woman was a murderer."

"Oh, Faith! So you persuaded the others to agree?"

Faith shook her head. "No need. We elected a forewoman—Jane—and she suggested a preliminary vote. Twelve not-guilties. We were back with the verdict in under an hour."

Michael pushed the half empty bottle of Chardonnay into the ice bucket with a practiced hand.

"Was that really doing your civic duty?" he asked. "I thought you were supposed to discuss the evidence."

"I suppose we decided that our civic duty didn't include wasting the court's time when our collective mind was made up. Anyway, that wasn't the truly remarkable thing."

Michael waited as Faith took a sip of her wine, drawing out the moment.

"Well?" he prompted.

"The remarkable thing was that as Jane and I rode down the escalator, she told me that Molly Jupiter had looked at her and mouthed 'meow.' And Jane remembered the time that the refrigerator door hadn't shut off the light because of a problem with the switch. It was her parents' refrigerator, a very long time ago, which was why she hadn't remembered sooner. Her mother discovered the cat playing with this little plastic switch that came from the refrigerator door."

"And 'meow' reminded her."

"Yes. And then Walter, who was right behind Jane, said that Molly Jupiter had looked at him and mouthed 'meow' just as he was thinking she was probably guilty. He realized that the scratch on her arm could have been a cat scratch—he said it looked more like a cat scratch than a human scratch."

"I supposed you're going to tell me nine more stories proving each juror was swayed by Molly Jupiter's eyes, and that each one took 'meow' personally."

"No. I was afraid to ask because I couldn't tell mine."

"She may not be the World's Greatest Psychic, but she has to be the World's Greatest Hypnotist."

"Possibly."

"Did it occur to you that the two women were in it together?"

"Of course it did." Faith glared at Michael, then took another sip of wine. "But I wasn't about to make that hypothetical case for the other jurors. It was up to the prosecution to prove guilt beyond a reasonable doubt, and they didn't do it."

"And you were really afraid that someone, somehow, would expose you. You wanted to end the charade, and 'not guilty' was the easiest way to do it."

"I don't know. I rather liked being Elizabeth." Faith looked at the cat, who was curled up on the chaise a few feet away.

"Good. That means you can vote twice in November," Michael said.

Elizabeth opened her eyes, her deep blue, protruding eyes, and met Faith's gaze.

"No. I got away with it once and I'm not doing it again." Faith shivered as she said the words. "Besides, if the district attorney comes up with new evidence, I may have to confess my misdeed. I get fifteen minutes of fame and the prosecutors get a second shot at conviction. My cat impersonation may turn out to have been a good idea after all."

Elizabeth yawned, nodded in forgiveness, and went back to sleep.

Not in the Stars

A Faith Cassidy Mystery

My first contact with a professional astrologer was almost thirty years ago. She was my neighbor in a North Hollywood apartment complex, and she liked to sit out by the pool in the evening while she worked on charts for her clients. I would carry a glass of wine out and sit at the same table, learning by osmosis. We stayed in touch, and I chatted with her about this story while I was writing it. In order to get into the world of astrologers, I borrowed Dane Rudhyar's The Astrology of Personality *from my accountant, who is also something of an astrologer. Both women got a kick out of the story—although they insist, and I believe them, that astrologers are normal people, just like you and me.*

"Well, if there's anyone who would think the fault is not in ourselves but in the stars, it's you, Bobby," Faith said, annoyed at having to turn her head and talk over her shoulder. She didn't like having conversations with people in the back seat of the car unless she was driving and didn't have an obligation to look at them. The need to keep her eyes on the road was deeply ingrained.

"That's not it at all, Faith, and you know it," Bobby answered. "I just want to know what's coming so that I can prepare for it, like having an earthquake kit in the closet. And learning more about astrology can only help."

"Besides," Michael said, "you'll be able to amaze your friends with insightful comments about their personalities, just from knowing their birthdates. Think how in demand you'll be at parties."

Michael was driving, and the need to focus on the dimly lit canyon road spared him from having to look at either of them.

Faith turned back to Michael, relieved that he had stepped in. "I don't think my sun sign says anything about me."

"You're a Leo," Bobby said, "and you like to be the center of attention. How can you argue with that?"

"What? You're reducing me to one trait? One superficial trait? A trait that doesn't begin to describe who I am?" This time Faith turned all the way around, clutching the side of the seat.

"Now, now, kiddies, this is all for fun," Michael said. "It was nice of Bobby to invite you, Faith, and you didn't have to come."

"And you're a Libra," Bobby said, "so you're trying to strike a balance between us."

Faith stifled the impulse to tell Bobby what she thought he was. Instead she eased back in her seat, facing the road again. This was a wealthy neighborhood, and she didn't understand why someone hadn't insisted that more streetlights be installed.

"Besides," Bobby continued, "it isn't all sun signs. There are rising signs, and moon signs, and where your planets are, and all kinds of aspects."

"Please," Faith said. "Please tell me Michael's right, that

this is all for fun, that you don't really believe that the orbit of Pluto, which may just be a chunk of ice, not even really a planet, affects your life."

"It is for fun," Bobby said. "Nevertheless, it works. Whether Pluto is a planet or not. Where Pluto is in your natal chart says something about you, but I don't remember what it is. I can look up where it is in my ephemeris, and somebody tonight will be able to tell you the meaning."

"Your ephemeris is that fat blue book you're waving?" Faith asked.

"Yes. You can find out what signs the planets are in at any moment of the first fifty years of the twenty first century. I'm carrying it everywhere these days. It's a great way to start conversations," Bobby replied.

"You know," Michael said, "this may be an example of Neils Bohr's famous dictum, that the opposite of a profound truth is another profound truth. The orbit of Pluto can't possibly affect your life. Nevertheless, astrology works."

"What? 'Famous dictum'? When did you start reading Neils Bohr?" Faith asked.

"Never read him. But a friend of a friend is writing a relationship book for the self-help market, and I was looking at the manuscript, and he used the Neils Bohr thing to talk about men and women. Our differences are more important than our similarities, and our similarities are more important than our differences," Michael said. "So I've been trying to think of other examples."

" 'It was the best of times, it was the worst of times,' " Faith said.

"Exactly."

"Turn right here," Bobby said. "And look for a parking place."

Michael turned right as directed. They had been traveling up one of the more tortuous canyon roads into the Hollywood Hills, and the right turn took them onto a narrow, twisting street with parking on one side only, the other side, with no open spaces in sight. Michael inched along slowly, looking for a driveway without a gate so that he could make a U-turn.

"We should have parked a block back," he said.

"Bobby, how can you tell where we're going?" Faith asked. "You can't see the houses for the walls and the shrubs, and you can't see any numbers because the streetlights don't illuminate."

"I have directions. There's a cul-de-sac somewhere up here where we can turn around, and the numbers are on the curb, so we'll be able to see them when we're outside the car, and anyway, we're going where everybody else is going," Bobby said.

What Bobby called "everybody else" was actually two couples slipping single file between the parked cars and the dark walls and walking through the gates of one of the driveways.

"They don't look like professional astrologers," Faith said.

"And what do professional astrologers look like?" Bobby asked with a sigh.

"I don't know. But not that normal."

"If you want normal, Faith, that lets us out," Michael said.

They were something of an odd threesome, she would have to admit, although both Michael and Bobby had a West Hollywood hip-at-forty smoothness, and she thought she herself could fade into a crowd better than most TV personalities who had been forced into second careers. Not that being a therapist felt like second choice, not any longer. Besides, she had always been interested in people.

Michael found the cul-de-sac, turned the car around, and started slowly back down the hill.

"There's a space," Faith said.

"It's a driveway," Michael countered.

"Yes, but there's enough room between the edge of the driveway and the car parked ahead of it that you could argue it's a space."

"We'd block half the driveway," Michael said, not slowing further.

They were almost back down to the main canyon road by the time Michael found a space he was comfortable with. He maneuvered in, and Faith sighed with relief.

Bobby led them up the narrow path that passed for a sidewalk and through the same driveway gate they had seen the four others enter.

Once past the wall, they discovered an estate that had been carved out of the hillside. A circular drive swept up to a two-story, brightly lit, white stucco house that Faith vaguely recalled having seen in a *Los Angeles Times Magazine* spread. Some favored cars were blocking the path to the arched front doorway, which had been left open.

Faith stopped just before they reached the lights.

"We aren't going to be the only non-astrologers here, are we?"

"It's too late to ask that," Michael said.

"Of course we won't be," Bobby answered. "It's mostly a meeting for members, who are all professionals, but anybody who's interested, and who can get an invitation, can come. Like the Magic Castle. I told you. Avery Whitlock set it up that way in his will."

"Who would have thought someone could make this

kind of money writing an astrology column?" Faith asked.

"Avery Whitlock didn't just write a daily column," Bobby said. "He was the astrologer to the stars—the movie stars—for decades. Nancy Reagan is supposed to have consulted with him on soul mate advice before she met Ronnie. Come on."

Bobby led the way inside, to a foyer where a table had been set up to block further entry. A gray-haired, middle-aged man whose paunch pushed against a green polo shirt smiled at them. The younger woman sitting next to him, who was dressed in a tailored pantsuit as if she had come straight from an office, looked too earnest to smile.

"Do you have an invitation?" she asked.

Bobby gave their names and explained that a friend of his, a member, had called to okay their presence. While the woman was checking her notes, Faith peered through the doorway into the room to the left, which was large and sparsely furnished, as if guests were expected to remain standing. There were a few groups of chatting people, but not as many as she had expected. They were also more ordinary looking than she had expected, with many of them dressed as if they had come from day jobs having nothing to do with New Age oracles. Her attention was caught by a painting over the fireplace on the far wall, a portrait of a thin, old man in a blue suit, white shirt, and red tie. Avery Whitlock, to be sure, done when he must have been in his eighties.

"Okay," the woman said. "You're on the list."

The man held out three sheets of paper, one for each of them.

"Here's a list of the discussion groups and the rooms they're being held in. Decide where you want to go, and come back if you need help finding something. Refreshments are out by the pool," he said, pointing down a hall toward the back of the house.

Faith started to look at her sheet, but Michael grabbed her hand to get her out of the way of the people coming in behind them. Bobby was already heading along the hall, and they followed him to another open door, this one taking them to a patio and a broad expanse of lawn with an Olympic-sized pool.

More small groups were scattered around the yard. A much larger group of people had gathered around a long table near the door with three large silver urns, plates of cookies, and cups and napkins on it, and an ice bucket resting on the cement at either end.

"Do you want anything?" Michael asked.

Faith shook her head. She pulled her glasses out of her purse to read the small print on the sheet of paper.

"Astrological psychology," she said. "There's actually a discussion group that meets on astrological psychology."

"And one on karmic astrology, one on special cases in horary astrology, one on the transits of Pluto, just in case you want to find out how that orbiting hunk of ice affects you. Here's one on sidereal astrology as the true interpretative tool for the New Age, whatever that means," Michael said, reading his own sheet.

"Did you think it was all fortune telling?" Bobby asked.

"Well, sort of," Faith said.

"You were wrong," Bobby said triumphantly. "You might even learn something at the discussion group on astrological psychology."

"Maybe," Faith said.

She stared at the paper, wondering exactly what astrological psychology was. Bobby tucked his ephemeris under his arm and fished around in the nearest ice bucket for two small plastic bottles of spring water. He handed one to Michael.

"I'm going to the one on compatibility charts," he said. "Sun signs just don't do it, I've learned that much."

Faith stifled a retort, and then forgot what she was going to say anyway.

An argument between two men on the other side of the pool became loud enough to catch her attention. One of the men was short and gnomish, with a dark goatee. He was wearing a well-tailored, silky jacket over a black turtleneck shirt. A purple beret was perched rakishly on a head slightly too large for his body. The other was a heavy-set, gray-haired man in a green polo shirt who could have been the twin of the one at the front desk. People all around them became quiet as well, listening as the heat rose.

"Avery Whitlock would throw you out on your ear," the larger man shouted. "He wouldn't have put up with this kind of heresy in his house."

"Whitlock was a gentleman," the gnome shouted in return. "He was gracious to everyone. And he must be spinning in his grave at the thought that narrow-minded, reactionary boors are running his foundation."

"Actually, Avery was cremated," a woman standing near Faith muttered. "His ashes are in an urn on the mantel, under his portrait."

Faith glanced over at the woman and was relieved to note that she was talking to someone else. The woman and her male companion met the appearance standard that Faith had expected to find in astrologers. The woman, a slender blonde with the kind of heavy makeup that doesn't really hide lines around the eyes, was dressed in several layers of leopard print gauze. Sheena, queen of the jungle, twenty years past her prime, Faith thought. The man, bald and bearded, sported an Hawaiian floral shirt and a bright green feathered earring that dangled from his left ear almost to his shoulder.

"The astrology that was good enough for Ptolemy was good enough for Avery Whitlock." The heavy-set man was turning purple.

"Are you suggesting that Ptolemy knew the sun was the center of the solar system? And he secretly discovered the outer planets? Avery's astrology was heliocentric, he incorporated Pluto into his charts, and he would have been open-minded where the influence of Chiron, Ceres, and the other asteroids is concerned. And you know it." The gnomish man wasn't giving ground.

"But not the Beatles! Saying that the cluster of four asteroids named after the Beatles can influence the development of musical talent is making a mockery of everything we do, everything Avery Whitlock stood for." The large man's voice was full of agony.

"Avery embraced Jung. He believed that synchronicities happen because everything in a time period is connected with everything else in that time period. Thus, the four asteroids were named for the four Beatles because they emanate cosmic rays that influence the development of musical talent, whether the naming scientists knew it or not," the gnomish man replied. "And Avery would have understood that. If you hadn't connived with the attorneys when he was old and tired, he would have made me the trustee, not you, and you know it!"

The gray-haired man stepped back, gasping, speechless.

The smaller man raised both fists in a gesture of triumph.

A few people laughed, and one woman applauded.

"Right on, Carlo!" she called.

The small man bowed in her direction. The heavy-set one turned and walked away from the pool, beyond the lighted area, still struggling for breath.

"I guess I can skip the discussion group on the influence of the asteroids," Michael said.

Faith nodded, but she was more interested in the couple next to her.

"How could you have married him?" the man with the earring asked.

"Carlo is brilliant, really. And I knew as soon as I saw his chart, with the conjunction of his Mars, my Venus, that we had been destined to meet, and that something significant would happen as a result," the Sheena-woman answered. "He was so difficult, though, that I made sure we got married when Mercury was retrograde. I knew I'd want out sooner or later."

"Seven years is a long later," the man said. "Although I guess it was a lucrative seven years."

The Sheena-woman glared. "I earned my money, Kevin."

Kevin leaned over and kissed her cheek. "Yes, dear. Anyone married to an astrologer who stakes his reputation on a comet hitting Rome, without bothering to consult Avery Whitlock first, has earned her money."

The woman jerked her cheek away.

"Avery adored Carlo," she said. "He was amused at Carlo's error over the comet and took the opportunity to point out that Aquarius was the sign of geniuses and fools, and Carlo was simply being both at the same time. And he did give us reason to believe that we would be the trustees of his estate."

"We? You and Carlo?"

"Avery saw us as married on the level of spirit, no matter

what we were doing on the mundane level," the woman replied.

"Is that why you didn't feel the need to save any of your earned money? You thought you'd have Avery's trust to loot?" Kevin sounded almost amused. "You were way down on the list, my dear."

Faith didn't hear what the Sheena-woman said next, but it wiped the smile off Kevin's face.

"All right, everybody," a man's voice called from the doorway to the house. "I hope you've all decided which group you're going to, because it's time to get started."

The Sheena-woman started toward the house, Kevin following.

"Where are you going?" Michael asked.

"Oh, the psychology one, of course," Faith said. "What about you?"

"That's the only one I have a prayer of understanding," Michael replied.

"I'll meet you back here afterward, then," Bobby said. "And I'll take notes on compatibility charts so that I can tell you about them on the way home."

The three of them held back, not wanting to push past the people who clearly knew their destinations. They moved to the doorway only when there was space to do so comfortably.

The man who had called out was the same one who had checked them in, the apparent twin of the man who had been arguing with Carlo. Faith held out her sheet of paper to him, pointing to the astrological psychology discussion group. He glanced at the paper, then back at her.

"Up the stairs, all the way to the front of the house, door to the right," he said.

More people had come into the house while the poolside

argument was going on, and now everyone from house and yard had converged on the stairs at the same time. Faith and Michael pulled back again to avoid the bottleneck.

"Do you remember something about an astrologer predicting a comet would hit Rome?" she asked.

"The fashion designer, Carlo Firenza," Michael said. "I heard he went bankrupt, too. Not exactly Nostradamus. Is that the same Carlo as the little man by the pool?"

"I think so. I wonder who the twins are."

"They're not really twins, but they are brothers," a man interjected. "Larry and Ed Martin. The one who acts as gatekeeper is Ed. They're the trustees of Whitlock's estate."

Faith flushed when she realized that Kevin was standing next to her. He was smiling to let her know that he hadn't taken offense at her eavesdropping, and was merely replying in kind.

"Thank you," she said. "It's our first time here, and we don't know who anyone is. I'm Faith Cassidy, this is Michael Haver."

"Kevin Solis," he said, holding out his hand to each. "I believe I heard you say something about going to the astrological psychology discussion."

"Yes, we did," Faith said, returning his smile.

"You will have an interesting evening. Sophia leads that group." Kevin's feathered earring bobbed against his neck. It looked a little less festive than it had earlier.

"Sophia?"

"The former Signore Firenza. She was a student of astrology long before she met Carlo."

"And psychology?" Faith asked.

"That, too," Kevin answered. "She knew one of Jung's mistresses quite well, in fact."

"I can hardly wait," Michael said.

"Then you'd best move along," Kevin said. "She'll want to start on time."

Faith nodded her thanks to Kevin and moved away. The bottleneck had begun to clear, and she and Michael were able to start the ascent to the second floor.

They hadn't quite reached the landing when a piercing scream from the pool area stopped the entire group on the spot.

A second scream followed the first.

The stream of people stopped moving. Faith and Michael were stuck.

"Somebody call the paramedics!" a man's voice cried.

Murmurs of distress began to ripple up and down the stairs.

"Does anyone know CPR?"

"What happened?"

"It's Larry. He fell and hit his head. They found him in the hot tub."

"Is he all right?"

"Well, no."

The woman in the tailored suit who had been at the front desk threaded her way to the foot of the stairs.

"Please go ahead to your discussion groups," she said, her voice loud and tense. "We'll send someone around to let you know about Larry after the paramedics have seen him."

"And Larry was . . . ?" Michael whispered to Faith.

"The one in the argument with Carlo," she whispered back.

The line began to move upstairs, and Faith and Michael were pushed up to the second floor.

A siren wailed briefly outside, ending in abrupt silence.

"I've changed my mind about the discussion group,"

Faith said. "I really want to know what's going on."

Michael shook his head. "Probably nothing, and it's none of our business."

"You're right. But suppose they were really arguing about the trust, not the asteroids? Suppose neither one was willing to let it go? I'll just feel better if I know it was really an accident," Faith said.

She turned sideways to squeeze past the people who were still coming up the stairs, and Michael followed.

Once she reached the back door, Faith felt a momentary lurch, as if she had gone back in time. The gnome and the large man were again arguing on the far side of the pool. But this time Carlo was arguing with Ed.

"You pushed him!" Ed shouted. "Larry didn't slip—you pushed him!"

"Larry was fat and clumsy," Carlo shouted in return. "Like you! Oafs! Both of you! I was nowhere near him! He fell!"

Faith looked around to see where the hot tub might be. There were steps leading up to a deck at the end of the house, and three people with worried expressions stood watching some activity.

"Ed wouldn't have gone anywhere near the hot tub on his own," Larry shouted. "You lured him up there and pushed him in! You hate us both!"

"Yes! I hate you both! And Ed wouldn't have done anything I asked him to do," Carlo shouted. "And he's bigger than I am! He would have pushed me in the hot tub!"

"Carlo! Ed! Stop it right now!" Sophia was suddenly in the doorway next to Faith. She paused until everyone's attention was on her, then proceeded toward the two men. "We don't know that anyone pushed Larry. How is he doing?"

"Not good," said one of the people near the deck. "The paramedics haven't been able to revive him."

"Murderer!" Ed screamed. "Police! Someone call the police!"

"Someone already has," the man near the deck said.

"Not me!" Carlo shouted. "I am not a murderer! Sophia! Sophia has Pluto conjuncting Mars in her twelfth house! Sophia is capable of murder!"

"And I was upstairs ready to begin the meeting," Sophia said calmly. "Whoever pushed Larry into the tub—if anyone pushed Larry into the tub—I didn't. You are the one with the most to gain from Larry's death, Ed, and you have Pluto squaring Mars, so stop the accusations right now!"

Faith edged her way toward the deck.

Michael grabbed her arm, but she shook his hand off.

"There's still one other person who has a stake in this," she whispered. "The other person who wanted to be trustee."

"And the police will find him," Michael whispered back.

"But the evidence may be gone by then."

"What evidence?" Michael said it a little too loud, and Faith shushed him.

The deck was raised about three feet off the ground, so that inhabitants of the master bedroom could walk out through a pair of French doors to the hot tub. Larry Martin's body was on the polished wood. One paramedic was on top of him, still performing CPR, the other one knelt beside. Several people were on the stairs, blocking access.

Faith stayed on the lawn and walked around to the spot nearest the hot tub. She bent over slightly so that her eyes were almost level with the deck. Although she needed glasses for reading, her distance vision was good, and she almost immediately spotted what she was looking for.

"There!" she whispered. "Caught on the edge of the tub!"

"What?"

"The green feather." She straightened up and backed away from the deck to make certain that only Michael heard her. "Kevin went into the house ahead of us, but he somehow ended up behind us when we were getting ready to go up the stairs. He's the one who confronted Larry Martin by the hot tub."

"And thank you for finding the one thing that connected me." Kevin had been part of the group on the stairs, hidden by the others. Now he was beside them. "I have a gun. Please walk slowly around the side of the house."

"You have a gun? At an astrology meeting?" Even as Faith asked the question, she felt the barrel jam into her back.

"I'm a reserve sheriff's deputy," Kevin replied. "I always have a gun. And I know how to use it, although I'd rather not."

"Why didn't you just shoot Larry?" Michael asked. He was trying to edge away from Faith, hoping to attract the attention of someone on the deck.

"Get back over here," Kevin said quietly. Michael did as he was ordered. "I only wanted to talk to Larry about the terms of the trust. But he turned on me, just as he turned on Carlo. He lunged at me. I was only defending myself."

"Then why are you attacking me?" Faith asked.

"Because I don't want to be connected with any of this. With Larry out of the way, I'll be named trustee, as long as there's no sign of foul play. I'm sorry to threaten you, and if you'll agree to keep your mouth shut, maybe we can work something out," Kevin said.

"I don't think I can promise that," Faith said.

"Of course we will," Michael said at the same moment.

"Around the corner," Kevin said, prodding Faith with his gun.

She had barely taken a step when something thunked into Kevin's head, knocking him to the ground.

"Good shot!" Michael called.

A fat blue book was splayed on the ground not far from Kevin, who was already beginning to sit up. The gun had fallen from his hand, and Faith kicked it away from him. Then she looked up to see Bobby waving at her from the second floor window.

"I'm a witness!" Bobby shouted. "He threatened you with a gun! I'm a witness!"

The crowd surged around Faith and Kevin, only stepping back when a man with a badge flashed his way through.

"I'll need statements from everybody," he said.

The statements took much of the night.

By the time the detective told Faith, Michael, and Bobby that they could leave, they were exhausted. They rode in silence to Faith's apartment.

Michael let the car engine idle while Faith gathered her energy for the short walk.

"I'll buy you a new ephemeris," Faith said. "And thank you for your help."

"You're welcome," Bobby answered.

"I still don't understand how you managed that throw."

"I played high school football, Faith, and I still play in an occasional pick-up game on Saturdays. And I was lucky."

"Lucky," Faith said. "Yes. All those astrologers were arguing about what was in whose chart, and stopping Kevin came down to a lucky throw."

"Actually, Sophia explained it from Kevin's chart while you were talking to the detective," Bobby said. "It didn't have anything to do with Pluto. It was something about Neptune."

"Well, knock me over with an ephemeris," Michael said.

"Don't ever say that again," Faith told him.

"Goodnight."

Many Happy Returns

I had originally wanted to write a novel about this woman, a novel of a twisted road to redemption after time in jail. But then I wasn't certain I wanted to live with a murderess with post-traumatic stress disorder for the length of time it would take me to write an entire novel. So here's her short story.

The woman stood with her toes on the edge of the cement, as far as she could get from the wire gate without stepping onto the asphalt drive. Her body was angled as if she were willing it to leave the spot.

She shifted restlessly from one foot to the other, uncomfortable in her shoes, the heels higher than she had grown accustomed to wearing. In other shoes, she might have started walking. She wasn't certain how much longer she could stand and wait, patiently and quietly.

The road in front of her curved and headed downhill less than a quarter of a mile from the fence. She closed her eyes briefly, to rest them, then focused again on the curve, not wanting to miss the first glimpse of the car. The sun was too bright. She wished she had asked for dark glasses.

"Are you sure she's coming?" the guard called.

The woman glanced back at him and nodded.

"I could make a phone call for you," he added.

"No." The woman said it too softly and had to try again. "No, thank you. I'm certain she'll be here."

"Do you want to wait inside?"

"No. No, thank you."

God, no. She didn't want to wait inside.

The sun outside was no brighter than the sun inside had been, she knew that. No warmer, no different in any way. Nevertheless, she was beginning to feel a fragile power from standing in its light, its too-bright light, and going back inside, even for a moment, even to cool off in the shade of the guardroom, would erode that little bit of strength.

For much of her life she had been powerless, never more so than in the last year. But now it was over.

A drop of sweat extended the dark circle under her arm, and she tugged at the lilac silk blouse, trying to keep it away from her skin. She had gained weight, overeating institutional food, and it was too tight now. The light gray slacks had barely stretched around her waist when she put them on early that afternoon, once she had finished packing the few belongings from her cell.

Food had been the only sensory pleasure available to her for more than a year. But that was about to change. Soon.

A black bus with a sheriff's insignia on the side came rolling up the hill, and a surge of adrenaline forced her back from the driveway, almost to the fence. The shadow of the bus skirted her feet. She looked up to see the bus pass through the parking lot, watched the gates open, then swallow it up.

Dark streaks rose from the silk around her waist to touch the ones falling from under her breasts. She searched in her purse for a tissue to blot her face, but she hadn't thought to include one.

The black bus had brought her up the hill a year ago. She had a sense of shifting reality at the curve in the road, even before the bus reached the gates. The stench of the other women in the bus, a combination of alcoholic sweat and poor hygiene, had been so overwhelming that she almost vomited. Since then her nose had become less sensitive.

She tugged at her blouse again, trying to make it fit, trying to keep the dampness away from her skin. It was over. Kickout day, she reminded herself. She had survived the year.

The scrub on the hill had turned yellow again in the September sun. She had watched it through an entire cycle of seasons, waiting for this day.

The sun was almost hidden, the dry hill beginning to darken, before the car she was expecting nosed around the curve. She recognized the silver BMW 325i even before it slowed, then stopped, in front of her.

The engine kept purring.

No one got out.

The trunk lid flipped open, and she heaved the suitcase in, fighting the urge to slam the lid back down. She closed it as softly as she could.

The door on the passenger side was locked. She had to wait for the driver to let her in. She arranged herself quietly, fastened her seatbelt. The blast from the car's air conditioning made her shiver. The damp silk stuck like glue.

She had to touch the surfaces—the silvery gray leather of the dashboard, the gray plush of the seat. She thought about closing the louvered vent but didn't do it. She would get used to air conditioning again.

"I'm sorry I'm late, Lynn, but the freeways were jammed."

The woman in the driver's seat kept both hands on the steering wheel as she said it. She looked straight ahead as she pulled away from the curb.

Lynn. Annie was the only person who had called her Lynn for months, ever since the last of her former friends stopped visiting. She had been Marilyn in the jail, not Lynn.

That was something she would have to decide, whether she wanted to be Lynn or Marilyn. She had a lot to decide, really, although most of the big decisions were already made, had been made a year ago so that she hadn't had to think about them in jail. She wondered if she could ever possibly be Lynn again.

She looked at Annie, the woman in the driver's seat, and decided not to bring up the name question. The identity question. Annie hadn't been perspiring, and her clothes fit, and her auburn hair had been cut by someone with a license.

Annie, her sister, who didn't want to look at her.

The BMW smoothly completed the circle of asphalt and headed back around the curve, down the hill.

Marilyn—she discovered that she thought of herself as Marilyn—leaned forward, watching for the first house. When she saw it, white stucco with red tile roof, just as it had been when she had ridden up the hill in the sheriff's bus, she realized that she had been holding her breath, afraid too much had changed, in just one year, for her to even recognize a house.

She wanted desperately to see something familiar in this decaying neighborhood of graffiti-covered garages and boarded-up gas stations. All she saw was one frail, ragged, brown-skinned man pushing a frozen fruit cart. She would have to wait.

They paused for the light at Eastern. Annie glanced at her, then moved into traffic and signaled for a left onto the freeway.

"There are a few things I need to tell you," she said. "The family has decided against a celebration. We felt it would be awkward."

"Celebration?" Marilyn realized that she had forgotten to think about what would happen when they reached the house. She had spent her first months in jail training herself not to think beyond the moment. It was only during the last week that she had allowed herself to remember the future. She hoped she hadn't lost the ability to plan ahead, the thing that happens to people with frontal lobotomies.

"Your birthday."

Marilyn shut her eyes.

"I'm sorry—I really am." Annie's voice rose. "Turning forty has to be rough under any circumstances, and this —"

Marilyn could feel Annie's struggle for control, but she couldn't find the energy to help her. She had to conserve her energy to hold onto that tiny bit of power she had received from the half hour of waiting in the sun. She leaned her head against the window. Her window. This was her car. Two years ago it had been her birthday present.

"It was all I could do to convince Karl that you should have dinner and spend the night with us. I'm sorry, I really am," Annie repeated. "I'll help you find another place to stay tomorrow."

"I'm not sure I can find a place in one day," Marilyn said. She wasn't ready to tell Annie, but she had another place to spend the night, a night that had been planned a long time ago. She remembered that—she had remembered it a lot the last few days, remembered that she had something to look forward to. She could feel the blood surging in her veins, and she was glad her face had been already flushed from the heat, so she didn't have to explain. "Debbie and Buddy will probably want to stay close to the school, and there aren't that many rentals in the area."

"That's another thing." The other thing had to wait until Annie was in the right lane for the Hollywood Freeway. "You don't need to find a place for three. Debbie and Ross have decided that they want to stay with us, and Karl and I are happy to have them. So is Meryl. She likes having her cousins living with her. We all think it's the best way to go."

Marilyn froze at the name Ross. Then she realized that Annie was referring to Buddy—her son, not his father. She couldn't think of her son as Ross. And Annie didn't know that she wanted a place for four, not three.

"Why? Why is it the best way to go?"

Annie concentrated on her driving.

"Why?" Marilyn repeated.

"Come on, Lynn. You know why. You murdered their father. They haven't forgiven you for that."

Murder. Both the word and the coolness of Annie's voice jolted her. It wasn't murder, Marilyn thought. It wasn't murder. It was voluntary manslaughter with the special circumstance the lawyers call extreme emotional disturbance. Everyone had agreed to the plea bargain. She opened her mouth, but there was nothing she wanted to say to Annie about it.

Annie glanced at her stiffly, reprovingly. Annie had probably expected her to cry, she thought, would have been happier if she were crying, but she felt too relieved to cry. Ross was dead, after all, and she was free.

"Maybe I should stay in a hotel," she said. Saying it was easier than she feared. "I need to talk with Debbie and

Buddy—need to explain to them. I could do that tomorrow. But maybe tonight I should stay in a hotel."

"Okay. If that's what you want. Where?"

"I'll let you know. Someplace where they will take care of me. Someplace where I can get a facial and a manicure and a massage." Did the Chateau Marmont have a spa? She wasn't sure. If not, she could take care of those things tomorrow.

"I don't think that will help you with Debbie and Ross," Annie said. "They're looking for signs of remorse."

Remorse. Marilyn had to think about remorse.

"I'm not sorry Ross is dead." She searched for the right words. "I know you want me to say I am, but I'm not. I am sorry I couldn't come up with a means of getting away from him that didn't include bashing his head with an iron sculpture. But I don't think about that night anymore. I haven't thought about it for a long time."

She had a flash of memory, of Ross, naked, throwing her down on the bed. Then another flash of Ross covered in blood, and a surge of joy. That was enough. She turned back to Annie.

"What did you think about?" Annie asked. "You spent a year in a cell. What was more important?"

Marilyn was startled by how angry Annie was. What did Annie have to be angry about?

"I didn't think about the past. I survived, that was all I could do. I wish we could go back to where we were, though. You and I. Can we be friends again?"

"We can't go back to where we were as long as Ross is dead."

"I didn't do very well, did I? Letting you know what it was like?"

"What *what* was like? Marriage to Ross? What's to understand? That he screwed around? That he had too much to drink a couple of times and threw you against the wall? I can understand that. Shit happens, and Ross was a bright, funny guy, but he wasn't always a nice guy. So if you had divorced him, I would have been with you every day in the courtroom while you fought for custody and child support. That would have made sense. Murdering him didn't."

"Voluntary manslaughter," Marilyn whispered. She would have said more if she thought Annie could hear.

"They could have had you on second degree, but nobody wanted the trial, least of all Ross's partners. Ask Karl. They just wanted the scandal to go away before it ruined the firm. Temporary insanity would have been even better, but the DA's office wouldn't go for it." Annie's face twisted. She concentrated on changing lanes on the freeway, then continued more softly. "People can't just kill people, damn it. We live in a society that's falling apart, and it's all because people kill people."

"I'm sorry you were hurt." Marilyn was tired of apologizing, and she stifled an urge to respond with anger of her own. That had been a useful skill in jail, stifling anger. It was one she had acquired as a child, and she had only lost it that single time with Ross.

"Unintended consequences," Annie said. "We all have to live with the unintended consequences of what we do."

"You're making it sound simpler than it was—divorcing him. What you don't understand—what I don't know how to explain—is how powerless I felt. Until I picked up that small iron torso and hit him. He looked so stunned—so incredulous—so amazed that I might fight back—that I had to hit him again. And then when he was lying on the floor—when he was powerless—I hit him again."

"Stop." Annie's face had turned white. "I don't want to

hear this. Please just sit quietly until I can get you to a hotel."

"But this is my car. Did you forget? I didn't. This is my car. I'll leave you at your house. And call you tomorrow. We can talk then."

"Oh, God. You think you got away with it. One year in county jail wasn't punishment. You think you got away with it."

Marilyn was silent. They were leaving the freeway on Highland, skirting the edge of Hollywood to get to Hancock Park. She wanted to see the buildings, the people, the trees.

Annie turned the car onto a street with houses set back from the street, houses with landscaped grounds. She paused in front of a gated driveway.

"Thank you for picking me up," Marilyn said. "And for taking care of Debbie and Buddy. I'm not sure I ever really thanked you for that."

"You're welcome." Annie said it stiffly, without looking at her. "You'll need money to stay in the hotel. I picked up fifteen hundred in cash to tide you over. I was going to give it to you in the morning."

She took the bills out of her purse and handed them to Marilyn. Then she got out of the car and walked around it toward the house, leaving the engine running.

"Thank you again," Marilyn called to Annie's back.

Marilyn slid into the driver's seat. She touched the steering wheel and carefully released the parking brake. She eased the car away from the curb.

Freedom. She could sleep wherever she wanted. Stay wherever she wanted. Starting tomorrow, anyway. She had definite plans for tonight.

"Mrs. Bradford!"

The voice startled her. A short, dark, middle-aged

woman in a pink uniform with two shopping bags at her feet was standing in Annie's driveway, waving. It took a moment for Marilyn to recognize Consuelo.

She pulled over to acknowledge the maid's greeting.

"Welcome back, Mrs. Bradford," Consuelo called.

"Thank you. Do you need a ride somewhere?"

"Just to the bus stop on Wilshire, if it isn't out of your way."

"No, not at all."

Marilyn leaned over to open the door.

Consuelo tucked the shopping bags under the dashboard and sat heavily.

Marilyn again eased the car out into the street.

"It's good to be careful," Consuelo said. "It takes awhile for things outside to feel normal."

"How do you know?"

"My nephew robbed a 7-11. He was in county jail for three months."

"What happened when he got out?"

"Nobody cared. Everybody robs a 7-11, nobody cares, except people who hire you. When he got out, he came home. His mother was glad to see him."

"And he promised her he would never do it again?"

"No. The next time it was an Arco AM-PM. Don't tell Mrs. Stenner, okay?"

"I won't tell Annie. Where is your nephew now?"

"Back in jail, waiting trial. It's bad, you know? He robbed the 7-11 because he couldn't find a job, and he wanted money for clothes and stuff. Then he had a jail record, so he couldn't find a job, so he robbed the Arco. What does he do next?"

"I don't know." Marilyn concentrated on the signal light, on making the left turn on Wilshire.

"Who will hire him? His life in prison, that's what he's looking at. His whole life in prison."

"I'm sorry."

"Could you maybe talk to somebody? To give him another chance?"

"I'd be happy to, but I don't know anybody."

"Mrs. Bradford, forgive me. But you got a year in county jail for a crime I would have got life in prison for. You know somebody."

"I'll try to think." Marilyn frowned, not certain how one went about helping a petty thief. "I'll let you know if I can help."

"Okay. Thanks. The stop is at the corner."

Marilyn pulled over and Consuelo got out. She smiled at Marilyn the whole time she was retrieving her shopping bags.

"I believe you will help, okay?" Consuelo gave her a little parting wave.

"I'll do what I can." Whatever that was.

She drove down Wilshire toward Beverly Hills, wondering if anyone she knew would help Consuelo.

Then she turned north to Sunset. She had a date, a date set over a year ago, a date to meet at the Chateau Marmont. Blood surged in her veins again, the feeling of being alive. The blood in her head, in her fingertips, in her thighs, was arousing her. She had to concentrate on driving.

The traffic was picking up, and she had to drive slowly. Carefully. She didn't want anything to happen to the car.

Seeing the hotel turrets was a relief. She eased the BMW into the narrow driveway that led down to the parking garage.

The young man in uniform opened the door and smiled at her.

"Are you staying with us?" he asked.

Marilyn did her best to smile back.

"Just for the night."

She took the claim check and left the car.

Dealing with the clerk in the lobby was a little harder. But the reservation was there, in her name, guaranteed with a credit card number, even though hers had been cancelled long ago.

"Do you need help with your suitcase?" he asked.

"No. Thank you."

The clerk directed her up the staircase to the second floor.

The room was disappointing. Marilyn wasn't certain what she had expected, but something with a little more glamour. A newer bedspread, better upholstery on the chair. And a little less street noise. Sounds filtered up from Sunset Boulevard. Still, there was space. Space to swing her arms. A bowl of fresh fruit. And a framed poster from the Matisse exhibit on the wall, one of the pictures he had painted from inside a room of the view out the window, and she liked it better the more she looked at it.

There were no bars on the window in the Matisse poster. The artist was inside looking out, but he could leave. Now there were no bars on her windows, either.

She placed the few items of clothing from her suitcase in the dresser, her toothbrush and makeup in the bathroom, and lay down on the bed, enjoying for a moment the luxury of being alone, knowing she wouldn't be alone for long.

In the morning they could make the next round of decisions. Where to live, how to tell people about the relationship. How to tell Debbie and Buddy. The rare moments when she had envisioned her new life, it had included Debbie and Buddy. Somehow she had thought they would understand and forgive, and she still thought that. It would take awhile, but someday she would explain it and they would all understand and forgive her, Annie too.

She was still lying on the bed, staring at the ceiling, when the telephone rang. It had to ring three times before she remembered that she was supposed to answer it.

"Lynn? Lynn? I thought you were going to call me at the office when you got to the hotel."

She panicked for a moment, struggling to recognize the voice, one she hadn't heard in over a year. But it wasn't Ross. Ross was dead.

It was Ed. Yes. They had agreed that he shouldn't come to the jail, but they would meet at the Chateau Marmont the day she got out. And he hadn't forgotten.

"Ed. I'm just settling in."

"Don't get too settled. I'll be there in less than an hour."

"I don't have anything to wear to dinner."

"Hell, Lynn, we'll order room service."

"I'll see you in an hour, then."

Marilyn hung up the phone. Ed Bradford was Ross's half-brother. And he had hated Ross almost as much as she had. That was what had first drawn them together. Mutual revenge against Ross for being Ross. Then it had become much more.

Divorcing Ross had crossed her mind, but Ed had argued against it. They had so much more to gain with Ross dead.

By the time she heard a knock at the door, Marilyn was showered and dressed in her one change of clothes. Another blouse and slacks that were too tight. She was annoyed that she had to see Ed with a bad haircut, no manicure, and ill-fitting clothes. But they had both waited long enough for this night.

"Lynn! You look great!"

Ed walked in and kissed her on the cheek.

His lips were full and rough. She turned her face, wanting more.

"Easy, Lynn," he said. "Somebody's coming."

She pulled back and looked at him.

There was a faint resemblance to Ross, especially around the deep-set eyes, the same ones Buddy had inherited. Ed's eyes were bright blue, though, and there was no anger in them. The suit he was wearing looked like one Ross might have worn, Italian silk, tailored to fit. Ed was shorter and heavier than Ross. But Ross would have envied his thick, dark hair.

"I've been called Marilyn for the past year," she told him. "Would you have a problem calling me Marilyn instead of Lynn?"

"Not a problem, but you might have to remind me a couple of times," he answered. "Everyone in L.A. changes something. You might as well change your name."

She smiled at him.

Another knock at the door made her lose the smile. But Ed had said he was expecting someone.

Ed opened the door to display a young man with a ponytail and too many earrings holding a tray with a champagne icer and two glasses.

"Come right in," Ed said.

The young man set the tray on a table between two chairs.

"Do you want me to open it?" he said.

"I'll take care of it. Here you go." Ed handed him a folded bill.

The young man glanced at it.

"Thank you, sir. Anything more, just give us a call."

He slipped discreetly out the door.

Ed twisted the cork from the champagne, poured two glasses, carefully letting the foam settle, and handed one to Marilyn.

"Happy birthday," he said.

"To freedom," she responded. "And to us."

He clinked her glass and took a sip. "To us. It's been a hell of a long year, but I haven't forgotten. And you haven't either, or you wouldn't be here. You'd be celebrating with Annie and Karl and your kids instead."

Marilyn opened her mouth to tell him that they hadn't wanted her, but she decided that could wait. They could talk about Debbie and Buddy in the morning. She took a sip of the champagne.

"I want to be with you," she said.

"Come here." Ed put his glass down. "Let's start the celebration now."

Marilyn took another sip of the champagne. The wine was cool and bittersweet and the bubbles made her nose itch. But she wanted more, she wanted more of everything. She held up her hand to hold him off so that she could drain the glass. Then she put it down next to his and held out her arms.

"Now," she whispered.

Ed took off his jacket and dropped it on the chair. Marilyn was tugging at his tie, then the buttons on his soft white shirt.

"Slow, kid," he said, laughing lightly. "I'll meet you on the bed."

Marilyn stepped back long enough to get rid of her own clothes, tossing them so that they mixed with Ed's on the chair. She reached the bed before he did, and when he sat down to get rid of his shoes and socks she began kissing the back of his neck.

"I've waited so long," she whispered.

He stood up to get rid of his trousers. Then he was on top of her, kissing her with that wonderful rough mouth, kissing her face, her eyes, her neck, lingering on her breasts, sliding down over her stomach, and the blood was flowing in her veins and arteries so that she could barely contain herself, forcing herself to slow down, not wanting to spend too much too soon, but giving in to the surging waves of pleasure almost at once.

He worked his way just as slowly back up her body.

"I'll get us more champagne," he said.

"You don't have to stop," Marilyn said. "Please don't stop now. I want more."

"We'll do more. But let's take a break."

It was only then that she realized that he wasn't aroused.

She pulled her knees up to her chest.

"I've gotten ugly," she said. "You don't want me."

"Lynn, honey, it isn't that. I do want you." He poured two more glasses and brought them back to the bed. He sat down next to her and handed her one. "But I'm not as young as I used to be."

Someone else had said that to her, those same words.

Ross. And the words had always meant that he was having an affair, had slept with another woman the night before.

"Who is she?" Marilyn asked.

"What?"

"The woman you're sleeping with. Who is she?" She brought the glass inside her knees, so that she could hide her body and drink at the same time.

"A friend. Someone I've been seeing. She's not important." His voice was tight, though, and she didn't believe him.

"Does she know about us?"

"No. No one knows about us. We agreed."

"We agreed to wait."

"Come on, Lynn, you didn't think that meant I'd be celibate, did you?"

"I thought you'd wait." She had to stop herself from screaming at him. "How are we going to look for a place to live tomorrow morning when you have a girlfriend who doesn't know about us?"

"A place to live?" He moved away from her. "I think it's a little soon for that, isn't it? I thought we were going to wait."

"I did wait. I did my time. And now I want to get on with my life. If you don't want to be with me, get out."

"Get out? You don't mean that."

"I mean it. I changed my mind. I don't want you after all." She began to sob as she realized it was true. "I killed Ross for you, oh God, I killed Ross for you. And now you can't even get it up for me. I mean it. Get out."

"Not so fast." Ed's voice was cold, unloving. "I'm not ready to leave. You killed Ross for you, not for us. Although I won't say I haven't benefited. But don't forget that I'm the one who brokered that plea bargain, so you only did a year. Let's not quite say you owe me. Still, I've looked forward to tonight, and I'll be really disappointed if you send me away too soon."

Ed's face had changed. His eyes had become icy with anger. He grabbed Marilyn's arm, holding on too tightly. And his anger was arousing him. Like Ross.

Her heart was pounding, no longer from joy, though, and she couldn't think of anything to say to him.

His grip was bruising her as he pulled her closer.

She forced a smile, stopping him long enough to place

her glass on the table. She looked at the champagne bottle, but she wasn't certain it was heavy enough. The lamp on the bedside table was a Tiffany replica with an iron base. The lamp might be better.

It would mean another plea bargain and another year before she was truly free. Surely she could negotiate the sentence herself this time.

"Whatever you want, dear," she murmured in Ed's ear.

She felt him relax just a little as they began to kiss. She pulled him close, allowed him to slide into the warm, moist place between her legs.

"Oh, yes," she whispered, as his thrusts became urgent.

Her right hand closed around the lamp.

Senses and Sensibility

Female PIs in the Nineties

From the time the first of the Freddie O'Neal books was published, I would talk to anyone who would listen—mostly at places like Bouchercon and Left Coast Crime—about taking a Woman Warrior on the Hero's Journey, using mythic images in a female PI series. Thus, when Bob Randisi asked me for a contribution to a book, Writing the Private Eye Novel, *I knew what I wanted to say. And I remain grateful for the opportunity to get it in print.*

During the years when my desk faced a wall, instead of a window as it does now, I had a corkboard at eye level where I could tack notes, cartoons, quotations, and anything else that struck me as at least momentarily inspirational. The arrangement was random, subject to the whim of the morning. Few thoughts remained tacked to the wall for long.

One of my favorites, one I have kept on the original three-by-five card with a tack hole through it, is from an essay by Natalie Shainess on Antigone, heroine of a Greek tragedy. The daughter of Oedipus, Antigone accepted a death sentence from her uncle Creon rather than agree to a blasphemous but politically expedient act.

"Antigone is not the average woman," Shainess wrote. "But she is what the average woman might become: a person of autonomy, high principle, not narcissistically self-involved, and not defensively suffering, but willing to take risks to live authentically."

I can't come up with a better description of a contemporary female private eye than the one Shainess has given a character from the 2,500-year-old Greek myth.

I wanted to start with that thought because more attention has been given to the female PI's debt of character to her male counterpart than to her place as a direct descendant in a long line of heroic fictional women.

All in the Family

The family resemblance between male and female PIs is real, of course. The private eye is one of the two distinctly American heroic archetypes (the other is the cowboy), and the only one that could easily accommodate a gender switch when twentieth-century American women began to break out of traditional roles. Or when, as Gloria Steinem put it, we became the men we wanted to marry.

The male private eyes we read about and admired were fearless loners, without friends or family. The Continental Op didn't even have a name. But each of them had a code of honor, a commitment to seeing justice done.

The female private eyes kept the fearlessness, the code of honor, and the basic idea of autonomy. But autonomy didn't necessarily mean disconnection and alienation, the way it did for the men. As often as not, these women have risked their fictional lives not for strangers, because they have nothing to lose, but for friends, because they care.

And this has been true virtually from the beginning, in

1977. Marcia Muller's Sharon McCone is considered the first of the modern female private eyes. The name of Sharon McCone's agency—All Souls—is a clue that things are different. Maxine O'Callaghan's first Delilah West novel was published in 1980. In that book, *Diamonds Are Forever*, Delilah solves the murder of her husband.

So for female private eyes, autonomy isn't quite the given that it is for men. Instead, it is a quality of character to be carefully protected. And through the tension between autonomy and connectedness, the female private eyes of the nineties are beginning to explore the question: What happens to the story of the hero's journey when the warrior taking the trip is a woman?

Heroine with a Thousand Faces

According to Joseph Campbell, the myth of the hero's journey occurs in some form in every culture. There are echoes of the myth in every quest plot, every story of a search for a Holy Grail. But the young warrior enduring the perils of the adventure is almost invariably male.

In this culture, however, in the last fifteen years, as women have become police officers and firefighters and attorneys general in life, fictional women warriors in great numbers have been taking the trip—in the form of female private eyes. The new PIs call forth echoes of classical figures such as Antigone, who gave her life rather than allow her brother's corpse to be desecrated, or the Sumerian goddess Inana, who went to the depths of hell to rescue her lost lover.

So what does this mean to someone who wants to write her own private eye series? It means that in the best series fiction, the central character is slightly larger than life—not the average woman, but what the average woman might become—facing ethical dilemmas and physical danger with equal courage, and developing wisdom through the course of the books.

Do I think reading Greek myths before you start is necessary? No, but I think it helps. One of the truisms of writing is that you write what you read. Thus, all creative writing teachers urge beginning writers to read good books. Walter Van Tilburg Clark, who wrote *The Ox-Bow Incident*, urged students to read a thousand words for every one they wrote. Clark only wrote three novels, though, and I'm sure Charles Dickens would have argued with him.

I read more when I wrote less. Other writers can do both at the same time, a talent I admire.

You can learn from reading bad books, too. But reading good books gives a writer something to strive for. So read mysteries, good and bad, to get a sense of what is going on. You're surely a fan, or you wouldn't be contemplating writing your own. Thus, you've read Sara Paretsky and Sue Grafton and Marcia Muller, and probably some of the lesser-known figures. (Maybe even Catherine Dain.) But you should also read fiction that has lasted across time and culture to get depth and breadth and bring something new to your character.

You may or may not have read something by Amanda Cross, who writes the Kate Fansler series. If you like hardboiled private eyes, this won't be your taste. But if you haven't read *Writing a Woman's Life*, the book written by Amanda Cross's alter ego, Carolyn Heilbrun, run right out and get it. Now. You will receive valuable insight into the character of the nontraditional woman.

You will also learn why we have tended to view the quest plot as male territory and the romance plot as female.

Heilbrun explains that young men have been encouraged to see themselves as the centers of their own story, as striving and ambitious, while young women have been encouraged to see themselves as the princesses waiting to be rescued by the Other, who is the true heroic center of the tale. She argues persuasively for more women to take the quest, as writers and their fictional protagonists.

Hear Her Roar

But you do want to start with character, not plot. Writers tell the same stories over and over, whether framed as quest or romance. Erle Stanley Gardner said that he never worried about plot because all his plots were the same—A murders B and C gets blamed for it. I've used that plot a couple of times, and I'll probably use it again. Readers knew they weren't going to get any surprises in Gardner's books. But they kept coming back for a beloved character, Perry Mason.

As you think about your own character, remember that you'll have to live with her for a long time if the series is a hit. Many writers start with an idealized version of themselves. I didn't do that because I couldn't see my real self—and certainly not an idealized self—dealing with the kind of physical danger I had put Freddie O'Neal in. So for Freddie O'Neal, I started with something close to what I would want my daughter to be. It was easier to imagine a fearless daughter figure than a fearless ideal self.

Fearlessness is important. Female private eyes have to be even braver than their male counterparts. A number of male private eyes have what Dick Lochte has called a "sociopathic stooge" for a sidekick, someone to call on for extra muscle when the going gets tough and the odds are bad.

But if *she* asks for help, a reader may wince. In the first of the Freddie O'Neal books, *Lay It on the Line*, I thought it was enough that Freddie had the wits to make a telephone call for assistance without her captors realizing that was in fact what she was doing. A fan told me how disappointed she was that Freddie was helped out by a man—and that was even though the man was an aging African-American security guard, far from the traditional knight in shining armor (and far from the "sociopathic stooge"). I've had her ask for help since then—balancing her autonomy with connectedness—but I'm always careful to make certain her competence isn't in question.

So your female private eye must be capable of handling danger by herself. And she will be in danger—your editor will surely insist on it. Or at least mine has. And other women writers have said that their editors have taken the same stance. Antigone must still be threatened with the tomb for taking on the forces of evil. Only now she has to fight her way out to come back in the next book.

What About Love

When you add fearlessness to autonomy, doesn't it become all the harder for her to have any kind of romantic attachment? Certainly. I think that's why so many female sleuths become involved with cops. There are advantages to the idea. The PI has access to police information that way, for one thing. For another, the police officer has a nonromantic reason to be there. No extraneous subplots necessary to deal with the relationship.

But the most interesting advantage has to do with a built-in tension between them. Here is a man who wants to save her from trouble—whose job it is to save people from trouble—and she has to maintain identity and autonomy against that pressure. It saves the author from worrying about a happily-ever-after book in which he becomes the center of her world, otherwise known as the romance plot.

Janet Dawson makes it clear in the Jeri Howard series that the cop and the PI can't live happily ever after. Jeri's ex-husband is a cop.

I've gone in a different direction with Freddie O'Neal's romantic attachments, but that has to do with my personal interest in reversing gender roles in the hero's story. As I mentioned earlier, the goddess Inana went through hell searching for her lost lover. This is a traditional heroic theme—Orpheus and Eurydice are only the most famous pair.

In *Lament for a Dead Cowboy*, Freddie O'Neal had to go through hell to save a lover falsely accused of murder. I used an Elko, Nevada, jail cell in a blizzard as my version of hell. An interesting thing happens when she finds a way to free him, however. He can't quite throw himself into her arms as they ride away into the sunset.

That left her free in the next book to become involved with a university professor who isn't stuck with traditional conceptions of gender roles in relationships. The mythic counterpart to that is the hero's dalliance with a nymph—Odysseus and Calypso, for example. (If a university professor who is open to nontraditional romantic relationships isn't your idea of a nymph, don't write to tell me. Write your own book.)

I didn't expect the relationship to last through a second book. It almost survived a third.

Other PI writers handle the tension between autonomy and connectedness in various ways. I mentioned that

Delilah West started out as a grieving widow who had to solve her husband's murder in 1980. Half a dozen books and a decade or so late, Delilah has recovered. But her romantic attachment to a real estate developer whose values are very different from her own assures the reader that Delilah isn't likely to remarry.

Of course, there's no law against a married PI. Some classical male heroes were married (Odysseus, again), a very few male private eyes have been as well (just last year Earl Emerson's PI was added to their ranks), and a number of contemporary amateur sleuths have sworn to love, honor, and cherish, if not obey. Nancy Pickard, Anne Perry, and Sharan Newman have all negotiated that curve successfully with heroines Jenny Cain, Charlotte Pitt, and Catherine LeVendeur.

Nevertheless, I think Nancy Drew will grow up and marry Ned Nickerson before Kinsey Millhone or V. I. Warshawski seriously contemplates marriage. For women, even more than for men, there is still a sense that marriage is the end of the adventure and the beginning of the second shift. We've seen that too often in the romance plot. Thus, I can guarantee you that Freddie O'Neal will never be worrying about getting home in time to cook dinner.

A reviewer of *Lament for a Dead Cowboy* commented that the mystery was more important than the relationship. That's true of any novel descended from the quest plot. With a married PI, the romance plot would be tugging at your ear for equal time. Unless you have Nick and Nora Charles as your model (and if you think that's a good idea, reread *The Thin Man* before you start—he was the professional in the family, and they both drank too much), some kind of commitment to single living is the way to go.

Cracking the Code

That brings us to the code of honor. Just as with autonomy and fearlessness, I think this is even more important for a female PI in the nineties than for a male. While there is a certain end-justifies-the-means ethic in much private eye fiction, I wouldn't try to take it beyond breaking into the villain's apartment and opening his mail, or tinkering with her computer files.

Again, this probably reflects a personal bias. Nevertheless, if your female private eye kills somebody, even justifiably, I believe that as a person of high principle, she ought to deal with the consequences. One of these days we're probably going to see a female PI with a sociopathic stooge—even a female sociopathic PI—but I'm not enthralled with the idea of a female antihero. Check out *Mallory's Oracle* by Carol O'Connell for the closest thing to a "good" female sociopath in print and decide for yourself.

The Rest Is up to You

Beyond those three qualities—autonomy, bravery, and integrity—you're free to make whatever choices appeal to you. Cats or no cats springs immediately to mind. I write that lightheartedly, but it isn't a trivial decision. If you have a cat, you have to use her. Linda Barnes tells of receiving a phone call from her editor asking if Carlotta Carlyle's cat had died. Barnes had forgotten to include the cat in the story.

I've heard arguments at recent mystery conferences that a new PI trying to get attention needs to have some sort of gimmick. A gimmick may help—the female PI novel receiving the most attention as I write this stars Martha Lawrence's Elizabeth Chase, who is psychic—but it won't eliminate the need for a strong, likable character in a well-told story. And Lawrence delivers these, too.

As for the story . . . the story is what you have when you add character to plot. Story is more than plot. Plot is A murders B and C gets blamed for it. Story is how your own very special detective figures out what happened.

Writing one novel-length story about your character requires commitment, and writing an entire series requires compulsion. There must be stories about the character that you need to write.

But that's a subject for another essay.